Pumpkins in the Forest

Joshua Shockley

Book Cover by Joshua Shockley
Illustrations by Joshua Shockley

Paperback ISBN: 979-8-9995236-0-0
Hardcover ISBN: 9798999523624
Ebook ISBN: 979-8-9995236-1-7

To my wonderful wife, Mary Grace
My parents, who always made Autumn an adventure
And my brother and sister, Caleb and Hannah
With whom I share many of my favorite Fall stories

Listen to the Pumpkins in the Forest companion playlist for Fall vibes while you read!

Contents

Read all the way through to see the full story unfold or pick out a chapter to get a quick dose of Autumn!

The Forest

To you, from a friend:

When leaves fall, it's impossible to control or predict how fast they float to the ground. They drift and flip and eventually make it there on their own timing. Why don't we accept life by the same cadence?

Instead, we rush so quickly through life that we find ourselves burnt out and desperate for rest, often missing the best parts of the world we live in. Then, of course, we over-correct, true to our own nature. We tell each other to *slow down* and practice *self-care* but just turn it into another task. This isn't new, though; I'm already aware that I'm too busy and that life moves too quickly. We seem to have figured that out, but now we're trying to figure out how to slow it back down and make real space for rest. For me, what *didn't* work was talking over and over about the importance of slower living and staying unplugged. Too often, the idea of rest and self-care didn't end up being relief, but instead it was just another item on my to-do list.

The same was true with beauty, joy, and peace. Suddenly these gifts became tasks to insert into my day rather than blessings to enjoy. Seeing artists and influencers on social media became another form of escapism to a life I felt like I should be trying to achieve. I was constantly being told to live a slow and simple life while in the middle of a loud, chaotic, fast society. I found myself year after year chasing peace and feeling more stressed than ever. It was just another lifestyle to grind for.

When I did find the rare moment of peace, I would sit with my sketchbook and try to draw out what life felt like for me. It often came out in images of dark, tangled jungles with tall, skeleton trees that cast long shadows. The image was confusing and intimidating, and I couldn't figure out where there was supposed to be room for simple peace.

Then, comes Autumn, that lovely season. When the first autumn breeze breaks through the noise, I find a moment when I can breathe easier. Something about this season seems to cultivate space for the slower living that has been preached to me countless times. Nature shows us that it is a time of transition, to be sure, but it isn't the same as the haphazard, chaotic change our lives often feel enslaved to.

No, this is a time for *peaceful* transformation, when greens fade into deep reds and oranges, the summer wind slows to a cool breeze, and sunlight even seems to fade into a softer gold. In Autumn, we seem to be able to settle into a new season of life through our relationships and the cozy rituals that ground us.

When September arrives and Autumn settles in, I find my sketchbook quickly filled, not with images of a dark jungle, but with visions of an enchanting forest. As I live through and reflect on the stories from this season, I find the peace and joy that I had been running after are more readily available. Nostalgia and beauty guide the senses toward natural warmth and light, even in the mundane.

Stories from this time of year are saturated with rich feeling. They bring that warmth and light to chaotic times in our lives, and they serve as a witness, telling others who we are and who we want to be. These are the stories that over time become part of us and make up essential pieces of our relationships with others.

Sharing these stories creates a special space for us to dwell in. In this space there is healing for both the storyteller and the listener.

As I journey through the Forest, I have an old tome of Autumn Tales that I bring with me to shine light into dark days. They aren't dramatic epics or confounding mysteries. They're normal stories about normal people, very much like us. Like many stories from this time of year, these are the kind of stories that you can sink into like a favorite reading chair.

The beauty of these stories comes in sharing them with others, so think of me as an old friend, recounting cozy tales and adventures over a warm campfire. As I open up the book, imagine a lovely, Autumn day in the Forest. Watch the sunlight break through the canopy of leaves and tree branches above and cast a complex pattern of shadows on the ground below, and the wind gently swaying the trees in peaceful rhythm. Pumpkins sit patiently, scattered around the clearing we sit in, and the bright colors of fall are bursting from every leaf in oranges and reds while soft moss and pine needles resign themselves to their usual muted green. The air is cool and full of anticipation for... something.

Through the trees, the forest appears to stretch on forever in every direction. Dozens of trees surround this small clearing, making it feel like a special, sacred place. Peace is at home here. A few leaves drift down from the branches above to join the dozens of others scattered on the ground below. The blanket of leaves is muted and rust-colored. They're dry and light - the kind of leaves that crunch loudly underfoot no matter how hard you try to avoid it. Poking up through the thick, leafy carpet are a few wildflowers. They pop with bright yellows and pinks everywhere you look.

The clearing itself feels quiet and peaceful, yet it's full of sounds! High up in the trees squirrels are running and jumping from branch to branch, slightly shaking each one they land on. Meanwhile, their friends jump around, crunching loudly the leaves below, sounding much larger than they really are. The breeze adds its part to the symphony as it rattles the leaves and blows acorns to the ground with soft taps as they land.

With the breeze comes an earthy scent that fills the air. The smell of pine trees and tree saps mixes with the dying leaves to make a cozy, natural essence that permeates every corner of the forest. It's strong but subtle and isn't too overpowering. Nothing here is manufactured or built; it's all grown and nurtured.

Presently you'll find the two of us on the edge of the clearing, under a large, maple tree, sitting in a circle of logs and rocking chairs gathered around a small fire pit. The logs are covered in a soft, thick moss, and the fire is steadily burning and crackling pleasantly. The breeze carries the sweet smell of burning hickory wood across the clearing and drifts the smoke lazily upward through the canopy of golden leaves.

These sights and sounds are a welcome home for memories and visions of Autumn. The breeze brings thoughts of friends and family and moments of peace shared with them. The scent of pine needles floods the mind with nights spent carving pumpkins and racing through corn mazes.

Everything works together in harmony to fulfill a longing for the season between summer and winter when everything slows and relaxes. The world around us lets out a contented sigh as the sun softens its gaze and allows bright colors to explode into nature.

Here, we find that when we sit still, peace finds us all on its own.

September

Into the Mountains

Oliver jolted awake to the obnoxious ringing of his alarm clock at 5:45 in the morning. His mind raced to figure out where he was as his dreams faded from his memory. He quickly turned off the alarm and saw what time it was. He sighed, reorienting himself to reality. Today, Oliver was going hiking.

For a moment, the warmth of his comforter nearly convinced him to stay in bed. He had gotten in late the night before, and if he fully woke up now, he'd be left with about 5 hours of sleep. Normally he wouldn't be awake so early on a Saturday, anyway.

He got up early enough during the week as it was, but his friends insisted that getting up before sunrise would

make for a better hike, so he agreed to the early start.

Now, though, he could almost be convinced to bail. If he hadn't travelled several hours to do this hike, he might have, too, but before he could actually talk himself out of it, he swung his legs out of bed and began hastily getting ready. As he started turning on lights to see what he was doing, he had to further reorient himself to where he was.

He hadn't lived with his parents for several years now, so waking up in his childhood bedroom felt unusual. Oliver thought it was odd how unfamiliar his parents' house had become to him as he felt his way to the living room in the dark. He quietly tiptoed past his younger sister's room, who he knew would be sound asleep still. Once he got to the living room, he slipped on his hiking boots and went over to start the single-serving coffee maker in the kitchen.

Oliver was never much of a coffee drinker, but the machine heated up a cup of water for his tea. Once the water was hot and poured into his travel mug, he dipped the tea bag in and let it steep for a couple minutes. Trying not to *clink* too loudly, Oliver stirred some honey into the drink and sipped it slowly.

He allowed himself a moment to sit with his travel mug warming his hands on the living room couch. It was nice to be back home, or back at his parents' home, anyway. Looking at the clock, Oliver saw it was time to go, so he slid out the front door and closed it carefully behind him. He tried to be quiet leaving the house so he wouldn't wake anyone inside.

Oliver was still rubbing the sleep out of his eyes as he stepped into the cool morning. He could see a few stars lingering in the dark sky above. Light was just now working through the thin layer of clouds that hung overhead. He envied his wife who would undoubtedly still be in bed across the state. It was the kind of cool September morning that was perfect for sleeping in and staying under the covers.

Knowing it was going to turn warm later, though, Oliver hadn't grabbed a jacket on the way out. Now he was mildly regretting that decision as he cranked the heat in his old Ford Escape. He carefully maneuvered between his parents' cars, noting that his younger brother's truck was already gone. *Leo must have had the opening shift at work,* he thought, taking small comfort that he wasn't the only one up so early.

As Oliver pulled out of the driveway, he suddenly remembered what he'd dreamt the night before. Hearing the car creak underneath him triggered the memory of driving the Escape while pieces of it were falling off one by one. In fact, he'd been driving to meet his friends, just as he was that morning, but in the dream, he had overslept and was running late. Being in a rush, he was driving quickly to try and reach them before they started the hike, but the faster he went, the faster the car fell apart.

Oliver felt his heart jump a little as he remembered the image of blue pieces falling off the back of the SUV and clanging in the road behind him. He took a deep breath, assuring himself that, despite the age, his car wouldn't actually fall apart. Probably. Oliver had a feeling, however, that the dream wasn't just revealing anxiety about the Escape.

Before he'd moved away, his car had often been the default adventure vehicle for the group. There were so many memories of them cruising down highways to hikes or kayaking trips, and he had missed driving his friends around for the last several months. He took another deep breath as he exited the neighborhood and decided to move on with the day, though. No need to dwell.

Oliver turned his attention to the world outside that was just now waking up. In the dim, morning light, he could see the leaves on the trees surrounding the highway were at varying degrees of transition. Some were barely showing signs of Autumn while others were fully orange with red at the edges. As he drove, the breeze pulled a few stray leaves off the trees above, and they flew past the windshield, drifting silently into the road as he drove on. The sky was quickly getting lighter now, and the sun shed golden light on the hills in the distance.

There we go, Oliver thought to himself. *It's a peaceful morning. Nothing to worry about.*

Oliver put on one of his favorite CDs, and it rattled off a gentle, upbeat tune that he had come to associate with the change in the weather. Even though the day was supposed to get warmer than Fall should be, Oliver let the music convince him they were fully into the season already. A light fiddle threaded the morning with life, and the acoustic guitar drew Oliver out of his exhaustion. The soft melodies wove the scenery together into a peaceful image that actually made him feel more grateful to have woken up so early that morning.

Oliver pulled into the parking lot next to the local bookstore. This was where they always met to pile into one car before they went on a hike, although it had been over a year since they'd gone through their routine. Everything was different since he'd moved away. Now parked, Oliver saw that he was the only one there, which was typical for their hikes, but this time Oliver felt a little more anxious about it, especially after his dream the night before.

He watched the sun rise slowly through the trees in the distance and continued listening to the album he had put on. It eased his nerves, but he couldn't help the nervous dance his fingers were doing on the steering wheel, almost as if they had a mind of their own. He thought back to when he was in high school and how easy it was for the three of them to plan a Saturday morning hike. In fact, now that he was thinking about it, Oliver realized he used to not have any problem getting up early for those hikes. For this one, however, it had taken weeks to arrange a trip back home for him to meet up with the others, and he had barely been able to get himself up for it even then. He just hoped the rest of the morning wouldn't be as difficult.

Fortunately, it wasn't too long before two more cars pulled up beside him. First Randy, then Marcus, of course. Oliver was glad for the consistency and was relieved at how easily they seemed to slip back into their old habits as the other two hopped out of their cars and into his Escape. Skipping morning pleasantries, as usual, Marcus immediately requested control of the music while Randy began talking about his week at work, being sure to share only the funniest stories of corporate mishaps.

They traveled the winding highway towards the trail they were going to, and each of them pointed out the same scenes and views they always had on a drive like that: the canopy road distilling the light from the early sun, a deer grazing in a field, a tree whose leaves had already started turning bright red - the sights didn't surprise anyone, but everyone took a moment to appreciate each in turn. Oliver was glad for the familiar rhythm.

As they listened to the playlist Marcus had chosen, a song came on that Oliver didn't recognize and he asked about it.

Marcus answered but frowned, "I found this band months ago, though, remember?"

Randy chimed in and tried to remind Oliver of a text Marcus sent sharing the band a few weeks ago, but Oliver was sure he hadn't been included in that message. He half-heartedly said he thought that sounded familiar and dropped the conversation.

This exchange prompted the nervousness to spring a little closer to the front of Oliver's mind, but he shook it off when a familiar song took over the speakers. It was a Whitney Houston classic, of course. The comfortable melody drew him back to the presence of his friends.

Oliver couldn't help but roll down the windows while they hugged the curves of the back road they were cruising. Immediately, three hands stuck out from the windows, surfing the cool wind to the rhythm of the music. A few leaves threatened to fly into the car, but they were quickly swatted away like it was a game. At one point, Randy rolled back the small sunroof and popped his head out of it!

"Hey, don't fall out while I'm driving!" Oliver chided, bumping him with an elbow.

He didn't hear the response but hoped Randy was being careful up there. Suddenly there were knocks on the roof, nearly making Oliver swerve off the road.

"Oh my goodness," Marcus rolled his eyes, "His hat blew off."

Sure enough, Oliver could see a small, red lump in the rearview mirror, sitting in the road behind them. Luckily, the road was abandoned other than Oliver's Escape, so he could stop and back up a little to let Randy run out and retrieve the hat while Oliver and Marcus shouted at him from the car - hoping no one would come up behind them during their 30-second pitstop.

In the mirror, Oliver saw Randy sprint over, grab the hat, and sprint back. Oliver acted agitated, but secretly, he was glad for the usual antics that were often present in an adventure for the trio. The remainder of the drive was pretty smooth, but the hat incident injected an energetic buzz into the three friends as they chattered away and listened to the songs Marcus put on. By the time they reached the trail, Oliver felt a comfortable warmth had settled into his chest. A wooden sign on the side of the road confirmed that they had reached "Mt. Unali."

When they pulled into the humble parking lot by the trailhead, the sun had settled into the sky and provided a slight warmth to the morning air. A slight mist still lingered in the lower fields nearby, and the dew on the grass was shining bright enough that your gaze couldn't linger on it for long. The three friends got out of the car, grabbed a quick sip of water, and bounded towards the trail. In the shade beneath the trees surrounding the trail, it was still cool enough that Oliver once again wished he had brought his jacket for the beginning of the hike, but as they got moving, he warmed up enough to forget the thought.

They started towards the simple sign that marked the trailhead, pausing to orient themselves. The marker confirmed the hike was a 3 mile "overlook" loop, and there was a small sign next to it that explained the historical significance of the area. A quick scan confirmed that the site was originally in Cherokee territory and was later used for the military, not dissimilar to other historical sites in the area, unfortunately.

They all took a glance at the sign, noting a few of the more interesting facts, reciting a few of them in turn. Missing from the block of information was the meaning of "Unali," and Oliver made a mental note to look that up later. The three of them finished reading the sign and continued their march down the trail.

The leaves were a little damp at the start of the trail, so there was hardly a sound between them all as they walked. Oliver could smell the leaves as they flattened them underfoot; the scent recalled the many times before that they had hiked similar trails. The same sense of adventure filled him as he took in the sights. Through the tall trees, he could see the hills and valleys that surrounded them, dotted with oranges and reds that were poking through the lingering green of summer. Seeing the bright colors, Oliver once again decided that red was, in fact, his favorite color, as he was often reminded of this time of year.

As the elevation began to climb, the sound of their breathing got a little louder, and the little clouds their breath created got more faint as the warm sun rose. The three of them had continued their conversation from the car, and at first there was hardly a pause between them as stories of the last several months flowed. Oliver hung onto every word from his friends, anxious to hear about what was new in their lives. He was so locked into the conversation that he hardly noticed the tall mountains peeking through the trees to their left as they hiked. Their breathing got heavier as the trail got steeper, and they talked less, saving their conversation for the flat stretches they would come to later.

Higher up, the leaves were drier, crunching loudly under their feet, filling the silence of the morning. Some of the leaves were already a dull brown, but many were a bright red or orange and had probably fallen pretty recently. Oliver's senses were full of the sights and sounds and smells of the early-autumn forest around them, and they all recalled memories of hikes from years ago. It was almost as if no time had passed at all - almost, but not quite.

Oliver's mind drifted as he analyzed the past hour of driving and hiking, searching for any indication that his friendships had faded at all, anxiously trying to translate hidden meaning beneath things that had been said that morning. Soon, the scenery was gone to him, drowned out by his worry.

Oliver got a reprieve as they got closer to the summit and found an overlook to stop at for a few moments to take in the view. Once they paused, they began talking again, and soon they were completely wrapped up in the new conversation. At first, Oliver just took in his friends' updates as they shared good-natured complaints about work and recalled funny stories and situations they'd found themselves in recently.

Oliver soon felt a surge of nervous energy wash over him, though, as he again analyzed each comment and its tone. *Was that passive aggressive? How often did they see each other now without me? Why hadn't Randy told me about that before?*

"Hello?" Marcus interjected over Oliver's thoughts. "You awake?"

Oliver refocused on his friends, "Yeah, sorry. What'd you say?"

"I said, 'How's married life?'"

"Oh, right. Honestly, it's been really great! Claire is wonderful, of course, and we have really loved our home. It's definitely a different life, but it's been fun learning our rhythm. Plus, we've really liked the new city."

Oliver's friends both shot him a smile back at him and simultaneously said how glad they were to hear it. They switched their focus, then, to be entirely on him and continued to pepper him with questions like,

"What do you like about the city?"

"Have you found a good coffee place?"

"When can we come visit?"

"Have you found any good hikes near you?"

Each answer came with its own anecdote and quippy comment that elicited laughter from his friends, and slowly, Oliver felt the tightness in his chest ease. He soon found himself speaking freely about everything from the several months they'd been apart.

As they rounded the last corner before the top of the small mountain, the view stretched out in front of them. The Autumn colors dotted the landscape in hundreds of trees, and a river snaked through it all, shining in the mid-morning sun. Across the valley, the mountain range on the other side quietly watched over it all. A gentle, cool breeze revived the energy levels that had dwindled as they hiked, and Oliver felt at peace. Views like this made him feel, for just a moment, like things could never go wrong.

Oliver positioned himself on a small boulder by the rocky edge (maybe a little too closely, if he was being honest). The mountains were astounding. As the three of them stood there in silence, what he really noticed, though, was the overwhelming quiet that engulfed everything.

At first, it was unsettling. Oliver had gotten so used to the constant rhythm of sounds of the city he and Claire now lived in, and he was not used to the prolonged silence that covered the mountaintop. The longer they remained there, though, the more comforting the quiet felt. The more comfortable he felt, the more he noticed the symphony of small sounds that wove themselves into the natural quiet.

Oliver heard birds chirping, leaves rustling, and their own footsteps as they shuffled around the overlook. Each sound stood out on its own, weaving together with the silence around to create a tapestry of quiet noise. Compared to the sounds of construction and traffic, it felt deafening, but it also felt very relaxing.

The three friends sat on the cool ground and passed water bottles between them as their heart rates slowed from the hike.

No one said a word while they sat. Their eyes were drawn to birds and squirrels as they darted across the overlook. Oliver found himself clocking the shapes the clouds made as they drifted overhead. Before too long, Marcus couldn't help himself and broke the silence.

"I've missed this."

Oliver just nodded, feeling a different kind of tightness spring up in his chest. He had missed this, too, and in fact, had been worried these sorts of memories might not even happen anymore. He hesitated to share what he was thinking, though. Oliver usually avoided bringing down the mood when possible.

Surrounded by cedar trees and cool air, though, he found himself feeling much like he had on their many hikes before: safe. Safe enough, even, to actually talk about what was bothering him. Letting out a breath, he started with the dream he had last night and explained what he really thought it meant.

"I've been worried about our friendship," he said. "With you all still living here and me gone... I don't know. I guess I just feel like I'm dropping out of your lives and that before long, we'll just have old memories. I've wanted to spend time together again, like before, but it's just so hard."

Oliver looked up at his friends and saw sympathy and comfort on their faces.

Marcus smiled and said, "Come on, you can't get rid of us that easily."

With that, the two of them took turns back and forth reassuring Oliver of their friendship and sharing their own worries. This hike had been for them just as much as Oliver. Right then and there they began to make plans for their next hike, and the one after that, and the one after that, and then they made plans to come visit Oliver and Claire at their new home, so he wouldn't always have to be the one travelling. They made it clear that they would not let Oliver "drop out of their lives."

Finally, Randy just said, "We are brothers. That doesn't just go away. You're stuck with us."

Oliver blinked hard to keep unexpected tears from welling up in his eyes. Relief was flooding through him, and he felt better than he had in a while.

"Thank you, guys. That really means a lot to me."

Clearing his throat, Oliver suggested they take a picture with the overlook in the background, so the three of them crowded in for the shot. Oliver already knew that picture would end up in a frame on his desk, not as the picture from their last hike together, but as a reminder of lasting friendships.

By that point, all of them were starting to feel hungry, so they didn't linger much longer before heading back down the way they came, now going towards lunch.

The sun was higher in the sky now, and the underside of the canopy above them was glowing in the light. A few stray leaves drifted silently to the ground, and the only sound in the forest seemed to be their voices as their conversation continued.

They wound their way back down the mountain, and the path split off in a few places. On a whim, Oliver decided to march down one of the paths in the direction they hadn't used when coming up. He motioned to the others and took off, feeling a little more lighthearted and adventurous than he had when they started that morning.

The three of them rounded the next corner and came to an old bridge that was laid across one of the wide creeks that flowed down the mountain. The closer they got, the more they realized the "bridge" wasn't quite what it seemed. On the opposite bank of the creek there was a large tree that stretched high into the canopy of leaves above, and at the base of the trunk, the bridge seemed to sprout out and arch over the water below.

The three inspected it closer and saw that where there once was a simple bridge, the tree's roots had sprung up and wound themselves over the old wood. Now, it looked like the bridge was practically held together just by the roots of that tree.

"This is so odd," Oliver remarked, rather obviously.

They paused for a moment, silently debating if they could trust the structure or not. Oliver finally took a small step out onto the bridge, and he was surprised to feel the strength it had. Slowly but steadily, he walked across, very aware of the lack of railing as he glanced down at the rushing water below. Before he knew it, though, he was across and hopping down off the bridge.

Back on the other side, Marcus took a cautious step on the root as well, and with a shrug, closed the short distance to where Oliver was waiting.

"It seems like it's fine, I guess," he called back.

Randy walked across last and joined them by the large tree. The tree was clearly old and seemed impossibly large for the forest they were in. If all three of them linked arms, Oliver wasn't sure that they'd be able to wrap around it even then. The large root itself was massive, too. It had sprung up from the tree and joined itself to the old bridge, winding with it all the way across, planting itself in the bank across. Oliver was in awe of how the tree had reached out to keep the bridge together, as if it knew how many wandering travelers would need it. He thought it was quite beautiful.

Not being ones to waste time, they snapped a couple pictures and continued quickly down the trail, but the bridge hung onto Oliver's mind for much of the rest of the hike. He hadn't really ever seen anything quite like it. He figured if he could write poetry, there would probably be a lot of content from that encounter alone. Since he wasn't much of a poet, though, he was content to ponder the beauty of small, natural wonders, excited to tell Claire about the bridge when he returned home.

As they continued to wind down the mountain trail, they could see the forest around them fully awaken in the morning sun. Birds chirped louder and squirrels darted in and out of the trees as they passed. Instead of the reverent quiet they began the hike with, they ended it with laughter as they hopped over logs and tossed pinecones at each other. The trio at last reached their ride once again, and they hopped in, ready for a post-hike lunch.

Now driving away, Oliver caught his breath and let his heart slow back down. He was among friends and settling into something like the routine they had always had. Some things were different, of course. He was different, in fact. He had loved being with his friends, but in his heart, Oliver couldn't wait to share his experience with Claire when he returned home the next day. He very much wanted to hike that trail with her sometime.

It was definitely a different stage of life he found himself in, but his friends were still there with him, as they always would be. On that early fall morning, the sun was warm, the breeze was cool, the laughter was contagious as it always had been.

When he arrived back at his parents' house, he was greeted by his energetic, younger sister, to whom he told in grand detail about his hike. When Oliver said the name "Unali," she immediately asked him what it meant, and he remembered that he'd meant to look it up. Looking at the search results on his phone, Oliver couldn't help but smile at the translation of the Cherokee word.

Simply, "Friend."

Over the stream
  Travelers go

Over the bridge
  To the tree

Over the years
The bridge grew frail

The tree reached out
And held its **Friend**

— *C.E.*

Autumn Breeze

Bailey sat at her desk, anxiously awaiting that last bell of the day. At recess, she had seen what a gorgeous day it was outside, and she couldn't wait to get back out there! The dull classroom she had been sitting in for the last several hours felt like a cage on a day this nice. The breeze was perfectly cool, and the leaves were fully in the process of changing colors. Bailey hadn't brought her jacket to recess (she hated wearing it!), but fortunately it was the perfect temperature to where she could warm up easily as she ran around with her friends, playing tag and climbing on the jungle gym.

Out there, Bailey had noticed a handful of leaves had drifted their way onto the playground, but the lawn crew had already taken a leaf blower to most of the area. The wind almost seemed to know how much Bailey loved fall leaves, though, and had brought a few of them back.

Seeing the leaves had made Bailey think about their yard at home that had the first round of leaves of the season scattered on it. This was usually about the time her older brothers would start raking piles of leaves for her to jump in, but this year that probably wouldn't happen.

Thoughts of leaf piles left her mind, though, when the teacher interrupted recess to take the class back to the cinder block classroom to learn more grammar and spelling words. The third grade had already started more difficult than she expected, and she could not wait to be away from times tables and helping verbs (whatever those were).

Bailey sat at her desk for the rest of the day as the class wore on, gazing out the window at the world outside. She liked school well enough on the best of days, but she was still adjusting. Her family was going through a lot of changes, and Bailey was having a hard time with it. First, her oldest brother had moved away and got married, so they hardly saw him anymore. Even when he was in town recently, Bailey felt like they'd hardly had a chance to hang out. Then her brother Sam had started a job and moved out on his own while and the youngest brother, Leo, had started a part-time job at the hardware store and worked *all the time.*

Of course, on top of it all, Bailey ended up in a class this year with a lot of kids she didn't know, so she was having to start new friendships all over again. Second Grade had been her best year yet because she'd been in her Aunt Cassie's class, and all her friends from First Grade had been in that class, too! They had so much fun, and she even saw her cousin, Ben, sometimes in the mornings if she went to Aunt Cassie's classroom early. He would often be in there waiting for the bell to send him to class, so they would play games or watch cartoons in the meantime. That was all different now that she was in third grade and in a new building.

Her parents assured her that she would at least still see her friends from second grade from time to time, but that wasn't a big comfort to Bailey, who had gotten used to seeing them every day during school. Fortunately, she was outgoing enough to make a few friends in her new class, but it wasn't the same. She was about a month in, and she still wasn't feeling settled. These were the things she thought about as she looked out the window during class, oblivious to the lesson her teacher was trying to teach from the front of the classroom.

Finally, at the end of the day, the bell rang! Everyone jumped up at once, and, despite her teacher's protests, Bailey and her classmates formed something like a stampede as they rushed out of the room and down the hall. Bailey split off from her classmates who rode the bus and filed into the Richland Elementary School gym with the other car riders. The gym still felt like a cage as everyone waited silently for their name to be called, but at least was a cage that was more spacious and had no math or grammar in sight.

Her mind was racing as she waited for her name. The teachers made sure everyone was quiet so they could hear their names, so the only sound was the crackle of the walkie talkie and the echo of the teachers' footsteps as they paced the gym floor. Even with the quiet, Bailey always worried she would miss her name, though.

Today was especially likely for her to miss it because she was so distracted. The gym door was propped open to the outside, and Bailey could feel the breeze leak through and see the sunlight pour into the gym. She got more and more antsy as her friends were called out to go to their cars. Just when she thought she couldn't stand another second of waiting, her name was called! She jumped to her feet and ran outside!

As she quickly moved across the pavement, she shivered, now fully feeling the cool, autumn breeze. Her mom would no doubt scold her for leaving her jacket in her Scooby Doo backpack that bumped along on her back. Stray leaves crunched under her feet as she crossed the parking lot and leapt into the already open van door. Heart racing, she settled into her seat and began recounting the day's events to her mom.

As they drove, Bailey took in the fall scenery. Almost every house had some sort of fall decoration up now. Some had cozy scarecrows and golden straw bales, while others were jack-o-lanterns and skeletons, grinning mischievously. The breeze made wind chimes sing on the porches, and Bailey thought she could almost hear them as they passed. The stressors of third grade started to melt away as they got closer to home.

In the trees she saw yellows and oranges and reds fly by and hit the van as leaves drifted to the ground. The brilliant reds faded into rusty brown on the dried leaves piled up in the yards they drove by. The autumn breeze had carried the leaves from their home and laid them on the ground in every yard they passed. Some people were out raking them all up now, and Bailey thought of jumping into the big, fluffy piles.

Once again, she thought about the leaves in the yard back home, thinking of her brothers who couldn't be there to rake them. She asked her mom if she would rake the leaves into piles for her when they got home, to which her mom replied,

"Oh maybe. Your dad's working late, though, so I'm making dinner and may not be able to tonight."

Bailey frowned at this and turned back to the window, not seeing the knowing smirk on her mom's face.

Soon, they were pulling into the driveway, and to Bailey's surprise, but not her mom's, there was someone in the yard starting to rake the leaves.

"Pa!" she yelled, recognizing the visitor.

The van door was barely open when Bailey shot out towards him and jumped into his arms! She lingered for just a second as he spun her around before jumping down and picking up her smaller rake to help with the piles he had already started.

Bailey's mom called out for her to put her backpack inside first, so she grabbed it and rushed to throw it unceremoniously into her room before darting back out again. Before she crashed through the door, her mom stopped her to force her jacket on. This mildly annoyed Bailey, but nothing could dampen her spirits now. She rushed back outside, now a little more insulated from the breeze, and she jumped right into the work.

Time flew as Bailey used her smaller rake to help Pa get the leaves gathered to just the right height, throwing them on top when the pile started to tower over her head. The sound of the rake whooshing as leaves were flung into the pile got Bailey more and more excited as they went. The rust-colored pile grew, kicking up the smell of dead and dying leaves along with memories of years past. Bailey was getting a little impatient but knew that time would make the pile perfect when it was said and done. After what felt like hours, the pile was taller than Bailey thought could be possible!

She stared up, in awe of the leafy tower before her. Pa Bill knew she wouldn't let a pile like that stay standing for long, so he interrupted the moment to insist on taking a picture first. From his truck, he brought out an old Polaroid and popped into the house to ask Bailey's mom to take the photo for them. Bailey stood as tall as she could next to her Pa, but she felt like the pile behind was still so much taller. The camera whirred as the flash went off, and the photo printed out of the bottom. With that, Pa put the picture and the camera back in his truck and signaled Bailey that it was time for her jump!

Setting her face with determination, Bailey got ready to knock the behemoth over. Pa gave her plenty of space for her stunt as she walked backwards several paces, crunching stray leaves that hadn't made it into the pile. Bailey zipped up her jacket for added protection and crouched with one foot forward in an attempt at a running stance. With the breeze at her back, she took off! She almost felt like she was flying when she flung herself up and into the pile of brown and orange.

The landing wasn't quite as soft as she expected, but she didn't mind as the smell of dead leaves again flooded her nose. She laughed as she started to get up and saw that the pile had been so big that there was still half of it left, and the other half had been flung in a loose circle around her, some of it still stacked!

Pa immediately went to work restacking the leaves, this time going around and around until what was once one big pile was now a big circle that created a make-shift fort for Bailey. She couldn't believe how quickly he'd constructed the hideout, and the walls seemed almost too tall for the amount of leaves there were. In the middle of her fort, though, Bailey sat down and relaxed from her earlier crash.

From inside the brown and orange walls, she could just see the tops of the trees nearby, shaking in the wind. The sun made the orange and yellow leaves above glow brightly. She didn't realize it, but she had forgotten all about those times tables from earlier.

Taking a moment to herself, Bailey laid down and stared up to the sky. The breeze was blowing big, fluffy clouds around overhead, and Bailey pondered each one, deciding what shape she saw in it. First an elephant floated by, then a pirate ship, then a whale!

Outside, Pa Bill leaned on his rake and chuckled to himself and Bailey called out to him what shapes the clouds were in today. Bailey's mom, Brooke, had sent him a quick text that afternoon, asking if he would mind coming over to rake leaves with Bailey. With two of her older brothers moved out and one nearly so, Bill knew they wouldn't be able to uphold the Fall tradition, so naturally, he obliged.

Bill knew the importance of Autumn rituals and how grounding they could be. For Bailey, with the change that is happening for her family, he knew she would need a normal day of raking leaves and enjoying the Autumn breeze. Though, if he was being honest, it was as much for him as it was for her. He thought about the times he'd raked up leaves for his kids over the years and savored every second of his opportunity to do the same for Bailey that afternoon. He could feel the activity wearing on him more as the years went by, but he hoped he wouldn't be too old to keep at it for at least a few more years to come.

Meanwhile, as the breeze blew a few leaves off the outer walls and into the fort, Bailey suddenly remembered that she had intended to demolish all the leaf piles! Determined to snatch victory from her leafy opponent, Bailey stood up inside the ring of leaves and crouched, once again, in a small running stance. She was ready to knock those walls down! She took a deep breath, planted her feet, and pushed off towards the tallest section of the fort.

CRASH!

It all came tumbling down!

Laughing, Bailey started to get up, but the leaves were suddenly falling back on top of her as Pa flung the leaves up again! Now giggling almost hysterically, Bailey brushed leaves aside as quickly as she could to not quite get fully buried before Pa relented and picked her up out of the pile and brushed her off.

"I have to do that again!" Bailey declared, smiling from ear to ear.

"Only if you promise to help me rake it up when we're through," Pa Bill laughed.

That afternoon, as the light turned golden with the sunset, they spent who knows how long raking the leaves up just to knock them down again. For hours they made tall piles, long piles, curvy piles, and even piles that spelled out words! Bailey properly admired each one in turn before brutally knocking them down. Pa continued to help make each pile with the same vigor as the last, only slowing down when Bailey decided it was time to destroy their creation.

Finally, Bailey had toppled all the piles her heart desired for the afternoon, and she sat down to rest on the porch while Pa raked the remaining leaves in a pile in the backyard. Bailey looked up again at the clouds overhead and saw that they were starting to turn gold in the evening light. The wind was strong and moved the clouds quickly across the sky. Bailey saw a few more leaves flutter off the trees and had an idea for how to spend the remaining minutes of light.

As if reading her mind, Pa was already opening their small shed and pulling out a diamond-shaped piece of blue fabric: Bailey's kite! She leapt off the porch and rushed over. Pa unwound the string and helped Bailey position the kite just right.

"Run!" He shouted pointing down the lawn, and she took off! The kite caught the wind behind her and sailed up into the sky, taking string from the small spool as it went. When it was high enough, Bailey stopped running and let the kite stretch higher as the wind took it further from the ground. Soon the breeze took it high above the trees and shook it gently, as if the kite were waving.

Bailey sat down in the grass and watched the kite bob and weave, now side-by-side with the elephants and pirate ships that drifted on the wind. More leaves blew off the nearby maple tree, and Bailey could almost imagine that the kite she held was actually one of those leaves and that she had lassoed it with the string. The thought made her laugh, and Pa smiled, thankful for the joy a little breeze could bring to his granddaughter.

As the day faded towards night, the wind slowed and lowered the kite carefully to the ground, almost like it was trying not to tear it up. The light was drained out of the sky, and Bailey was called in for dinner. Tired out, Bailey relented to clean up for the meal while Pa gathered straggling leaves in their final piles. Before he left, he made sure to stop in and give Bailey the picture from earlier that had finished developing.

That night, she would stare at that photo for a long time before finally finding a place for it among her most treasured possessions, almost forgetting all about the troubles of starting a new school year and simply being happy about Fall coming once again. As she drifted off to sleep, Bailey's thoughts were of how she would tell her friends about elephants in the sky and lassoing leaves out of the air.

Softly the breeze tugs at the leaves
Softly it pulls them to the ground
Softly it lifts them into the air
Softly they float back again

Gently the string fights the wind
Gently they work together
Gently the kite flies high above
Gently it draws out a smile

-C.E.

The Secret Library

Blake had been in Arborville for several months now, but he still felt out of place as he took his afternoon walk around the small town square. He had moved to the town over the summer ahead of the start of his new graduate program at the local university, but he was not very good at exploring his surroundings on his own.

The first couple of months were spent settling and resettling his new apartment as he hung pictures, then rehung them in different places according to the ever-changing arrangement of the furniture. It was a small space that didn't have much room on the walls to work with, so there weren't many possible arrangements for the posters and paintings he brought with him from undergrad. Nothing really felt right in the space, though, and he often ended up taking most of it down anyway, leaving the walls mostly blank. He just could not seem to get comfortable in his new home.

When the school year started, his schedule felt more and more packed to the point of feeling like he didn't have time to even sleep, much less venture into the town to find something to do in the free time he didn't even have. His hobby was studying, and he was fine with that. As September set in, though, the workload felt gradually lighter, and he found a good rhythm with his responsibilities. Soon, he actually did have free time but didn't have anything to do with it.

It was during a call from home that his mom told him directly that he should explore Arborville more. She had actually gone to undergrad at the same university Blake was at and loved the college town that had sprung up around it. She was sure it had changed a lot over the years, but there were several things she listed for Blake to check out, anyway. Most of the suggestions did not particularly interest him. She mentioned a bowling alley, a skating rink, a local boutique, and - a *bookstore!* Blake focused back in for the description of the shop his mom had apparently frequented when she lived there.

"Oh, you'd love this place!" She insisted, "It was such a cozy, little shop to go spend time in, and you can find good books for real cheap!"

Trying not to let on his excitement, Blake mumbled out that he'd try to give it a look when he got a chance and moved on. As the conversation continued, though, his mind drifted back to that bookshop, wondering what finds he might stumble across there.

Blake absolutely loved books. He usually was juggling two or three at a time with several more queued at any given moment, but since he started his grad program, he'd sunk into a bit of a reading funk. A major reason for this was that his supply was cut off now that he wasn't home.

For undergrad, he had attended the local university back where his family still lived, so he had uninterrupted access to the local bookstore that he had grown attached to all throughout high school. Now, hours away from home, he hadn't had the heart to look for a replacement. After a few months without a regular shop to go to, though, his mom's recommendation rang in his ears and piqued his curiosity.

Meanwhile, his mom was talking about some of the changes at home now that Blake wasn't there. With him gone and his younger brother staying busy on his own with school and his new job, Blake's parents had more time to do things on their own, like an upcoming camping trip, apparently. She sounded a little nervous to go camping, but Blake knew his mom would also really enjoy it. He felt a slight pang thinking about how much he would also enjoy a camping trip with his family, but things were different now that he was away. He hoped he could settle into his new home soon.

Over the next couple of weeks as his workload lightened up, he decided to spend an hour or so in the afternoons walking down the sidewalk to the town square that was near his apartment. The cooling air of late September made it pleasant to be outside, and as he walked day after day, he passed the shop that his mom described, pleasantly surprised that it was still open after all these years. A couple weeks passed after he first found it, but he still hadn't gone in.

He kept thinking back to the Red Dragon Bookstore back home, almost sure that this new place wouldn't hold up. Not that it could with the amount of nostalgia his home bookstore carried for him. He spent so many hours sitting in the cozy store with his younger brother, Caleb, reading books and playing games. They practically grew up there. He had dozens of warm memories of the two of them sitting in their usual nook, tearing through whatever book they were working on at the time. It was the perfect retreat.

Still, despite his impossibly high standards for a proper bookshop, Blake found himself outside the shop on a particularly windy day, browsing some of the books in the window display. For the hundredth time, Blake read the wooden sign hanging above the glass door that read "Tome Solomon." He frowned to himself, thinking how ominous that sounded. The wind picked up a little, and a chill ran through him.

Overhead some darker clouds blew in front of the sun, and the sky got darker. Blake shivered at the sudden coolness and was about to move on when-

"Hey!"

Blake jumped and turned around to see one of his classmates walking up to him.

"Oh, hey!" he responded quickly, trying to regain his composure. "Sarah, right?"

"Yeah, Blake?"

"That's me."

Sarah walked up beside him and joined him in staring at the storefront.

"Have you been inside yet?" Sarah asked, to which Blake shook his head.

"Not yet. Maybe I'll stop in sometime."

Without another word, Sarah walked toward the door and pulled it open, jingling the bell that hung inside as she did. She stopped and turned around.

"You coming?"

After weeks of walking by the shop, just like that, Blake was finally slipping in out of the windy afternoon. Inside, it was quiet. It was mostly lit by natural light aside from a few warm lamps set up on a few of the dozens of bookshelves that filled the room. The walls were made of exposed brick that had a muted, red color.

Blake was stunned by how much larger the space seemed to be on the inside. The dark wooden bookshelves stretched into long aisles that twisted and turned away from him, forming a maze of literature. There was also a small counter near the front window that had a register on it, but there was no one around. In fact, as he looked around, Blake realized he didn't know where Sarah went. He slowly started walking down the first aisle in front of him, scanning through the shelves as he went.

"Sarah?" He called, trying to keep his voice down.

She wasn't that far ahead of me, right? He thought to himself.

As he continued through the shelves, he wound deeper and deeper through the labyrinth, stopping here and there to inspect a volume that caught his eye. He found copies of some of his favorite books, some that were even special editions, and they were practically begging him to take them home, but he left them where they were, for now.

There were a few books he came across that he had never heard of, and he found himself getting lost reading snippets of them for several minutes before taking a mental note of the title and moving on. As he got towards the far end of the maze of bookshelves, he began to hear faint music spilling over the shelves. Curious, he continued on, trying to take the right turns to take him towards the music.

Finally, Blake turned a corner that led him to a small staircase that climbed to a second-floor landing just above the shelves on the ground floor. Blake cautiously placed his foot on the plush carpet that covered the stairs, eliciting a loud creak from the wood beneath. He paused for a moment, feeling like he was trespassing. He debated for a minute with himself, but his curiosity was pushing him forward. He was about to start climbing again when he got startled by a voice from behind him, for the second time that day.

"There you are!"

Blake jumped a little and turned to see Sarah turning the corner he had a minute before.

"I was beginning to wonder if you had actually come in." She said, smiling at him as if they were old friends playing hide-n-seek. Blake breathed out and returned the smile.

"And I thought you had already gotten yourself lost. Come on, I was just about to see what's up here!" With that he led the way up the stairs to the landing above, feeling less cautious than he had a moment before.

The stairs led him to a floor that opened up to a large space overlooking the floor below. Blake looked over the balcony and examined the paths he could now clearly see between the bookcases on the ground floor. Turning, he and Sarah silently took in the rest of the space that was in front of them.

The brick walls were lined with heavy-looking shelves like the ones below, but the rest of the room was open, except for a couch and a couple of large chairs gathered together by the large window on the wall opposite the staircase. The light spilling in from the window was bright and lit up the whole area, but there was an old chandelier that hung from the tall ceiling to disperse the shadows that would have lingered otherwise. In the corner, by the railing that overlooked the ground floor, there sat a simple turntable that was humming a pleasant tune.

Blake and Sarah walked over to the nearest wall of books without a word and began searching through the neatly-shelved residents. Blake typically considered himself an extrovert, but he found himself having a hard time starting a conversation. He scanned over several books without really reading the words on the spines, trying to decide if he should say anything or not. Meanwhile, Sarah found a book that she apparently recognized and yanked it off the shelf excitedly.

"Here you are!" She whispered. Blake saw the opening for conversation and took his chance.

"What is it?"

This prompted a long explanation from Sarah about the book series she had been working through and how anxiously she had been wanting to read the next one. Blake had expected a fairly short response, but Sarah continued to give him as much detail as she could about the series and what she loved about it (without spoiling anything, of course). She went on for several minutes, and Blake hung onto every word, admiring her enthusiasm for the fantastical world of the books she had been reading.

Soon, of course, she talked Blake into picking up the first book in the series, and the two of them wandered over to the chairs to dive in. They made a valiant effort, but soon, the books were left sitting on the small coffee table between the chairs as they continued discussing their favorite stories, classes, and just about everything else under the sun. Blake shared the challenges of being away from home and his brother, and Sarah talked about how hard her classes had been so far that semester. They both found a moment of calm, though, surrounded by rows of books and gentle music.

Eventually, their conversation turned to the bookstore they had settled into and how oddly quiet it felt. Inevitably, their combined restlessness and curiosity prompted them to get up and explore more. Together they browsed each shelf that surrounded the landing, noting the way the books seemed to be organized more by idea than anything else. As they browsed, Blake noticed one bookcase that was a little different from the others.

This one was crafted with a heavier, older-looking wood that subtly stood out from the polished material that the others were made of. The books on this one were all classics like *Journey to the Center of the Earth* and *The Count of Monte Cristo*. Sarah was particularly intrigued by this bookcase and passed her fingertips over each book's spine, reverently. She made a point to tap each one she had read before, specifically mentioning each aloud as she did. Blake had only read a few of them, but he made sure to jump in when Sarah mentioned one they had overlapped with.

As Blake scanned the shelves, one book stood out to him from the rest. He wasn't sure why, but *Alexandria* seemed different from the other books. He thought maybe it was just a classic he wasn't familiar with (which wouldn't be too extraordinary), but when he said something to Sarah, she confirmed that it was not one she had heard of either. Other than that, the faded, red book didn't stand out visibly and could have easily been missed.

Blake reached out to grab it, and he felt a slight resistance as he started to pull it off the shelf. His heart leapt as he processed what he was seeing, and the book leaned back at an angle. Blake felt a mechanism click as he pulled on it. *A secret switch!*

Suddenly the bookcase began to swing outward, forcing Sarah and Blake to jump out of the way. They both stood there for a beat, mouths open as they stared into the open doorway. The initial shock passed, and they started jumping and celebrating at the excitement of discovering a secret room! They quickly rushed in without so much as a thought between them. Inside, they found a large, round room that was filled with an other-worldly purple light that poured in from a large, circular stained-glass window above them. The light revealed tall bookcases that stretched all the way around the perimeter of the room. Each shelf was weighed down with books of all shapes and sizes.

They approached the shelves and noticed how old the books looked, much older than anything that they'd seen so far. The tomes rested on the shelves, watching respectfully as the two newcomers excitedly took them all in.

Beyond that, the bookcases themselves were much more ornate than the ones outside. These had intricate carvings of vines and leaves that wound over each shelf and continued all the way around the room, as if they had truly grown there between the books. The designs were painted a deep, rich green with gold accents that glowed in the light from the window. Sarah and Blake spun in a circle with gaping mouths. They couldn't believe their find!

Blake wondered to himself if his mom had ever found this room when she was in college, or if the secret room even existed at the time. If she knew about it, she hadn't hinted at it at all. Although, it wouldn't have surprised Blake if she had left it up to him to find on his own.

Outside the secret room, Blake heard the record stop, and he was very aware of how quiet it was without the music. Then came footsteps from the staircase, slowly getting closer as the wooden steps creaked one at a time. It was then that Blake's mind began racing, now considering the possibility that they were not supposed to be in there. He tried to calm himself, but he could hear how loud his breathing was in the silence left by the music's absence.

His heart pounded in his chest as the footsteps reached the second floor and began moving towards the door they had just come through. Neither of them said a word, but Blake could tell Sarah was also nervous by how fast she had started breathing, too. The footsteps reached the door and paused a second before a face popped around the corner, causing Sarah and Blake to jump, in spite of themselves.

"Hello! It looks like you found our little secret!"

The voice came from a small lady with a warm smile that stood in the doorway. Blake's best estimate put her anywhere from 45 to 95 years old. That is, he genuinely could not tell. She had a gentle expression that relaxed the two trespassers before they even had the chance to worry much more about their unintended crime. Relaxed though they were, they simultaneously started to explain how they stumbled across the room, as apologetically as they could. The woman waved their apologies aside and interrupted saying,

"Oh, don't worry about it! We love when visitors find our little oasis." Gesturing around, she continued, "Isn't it cool!"

Flabbergasted, Blake nodded.

"What, exactly, is this place?"

The woman smiled again. "This is our Special Collection that we keep tucked away. It includes first edition copies of many books that we've collected over the years, as well as a few particularly rare ones that are hard to come by."

Blake noticed Sarah perk up a little at the mention of first edition books.

"First editions?" She asked, looking around. "Of which books?"

"Oh, all sorts! We have some Tolkien, some Dickens, and all sorts of others. Go on, take a look!" The woman gestured around.

"I'm Ms. Solomon, by the way. I own the shop."

"Good to meet you Ms. Solomon. I'm Blake."

"Oh, and I'm Sarah," but Sarah was already fully captivated by the volumes she found on the shelves around them as she continued browsing.

Blake started to join her, but he had a few questions first.

"So, is this part of the shop, then?"

Ms. Solomon paused a moment before answering. "No, not exactly. We don't sell these, but we do let people borrow them, from time to time. This is more of a library, I suppose."

At that comment, Sarah whipped her head back towards Blake and Ms. Solomon with stars in her eyes before resuming her search.

"So, the hidden door is to protect it all?" Blake asked.

Ms. Solomon smirked a little before answering, "Well, to tell you the truth, that's just a bit of fun. It does naturally deter the more casual readers from finding the room, though."

Blake chuckled at that, thinking he liked this lady's style. With that, he joined Sarah at the nearest bookcase. Overhead, the sun peaked out from the clouds and bathed the room in brighter, purple light through the stained glass. Blake could hear stray leaves falling and blowing on the roof above, and he felt a combination of peace and excitement as he and Sarah searched.

"Take all the time you need, dears," Ms. Solomon called out as she left the room. The music began again outside, indicating that she had flipped the record over on the player.

Meanwhile, Sarah had found something she liked and called Blake over to see. It was an old, ornate copy of Don Quijote that Sarah had carefully pulled off the shelf and was bringing over to a nearby desk with a small lamp. She gingerly opened up the book, releasing a small plume of dust, and began pouring over the contents.

"Do you speak Spanish?" Blake asked, struggling to find any meaning from the words on the page.

"A little," she replied, "Though this is pretty old Spanish, so I'm having a hard time getting anything. Still, it's so cool!"

Blake agreed and poured over the text with her, admiring the artifact. They repeated this process with many other volumes from the shelves of the hidden room before noticing the time and deciding to retire for the afternoon. They carefully replaced the bookcase/door and corrected the position of *Alexandria*. They grabbed the books they had abandoned on the coffee table earlier and made their way back downstairs and through the maze below.

They found Ms. Solomon at the front desk, reading a book, of course.

"Did you find everything, alright?" She asked excitedly.

"We did!" Sarah said. "We decided not to borrow anything today, but we will definitely be coming back!"

"Oh good! I'm glad you all enjoyed yourselves," Ms. Solomon said as she scanned Sarah's book. "You know, if you come back on Saturday morning, you can join the book club that meets here!"

Blake imagined sitting upstairs in a cozy chair by the window with Sarah talking about what they were reading and smiled to himself. Simultaneously, they told Ms. Solomon they would love to.

They both checked out their books and waved goodbye as they stepped back into the autumn day. Blake thought the chilly breeze that had come through earlier now felt a little more refreshing than it had before.

"Well," he started, "I guess I'll see you in cla-"

"Hold up! Let me give you my number before I forget!" Sarah interrupted.

Feeling flustered in spite of himself, Blake obliged and handed it over. She quickly typed the numbers in and handed it back.

"If I don't see you before, text me about book club on Saturday. It sounds like a lot of fun!"

Blake blinked and smiled, "Yes! I will definitely do that."

With that, Sarah walked away as suddenly as she had shown up earlier that afternoon, this time waving as she rounded the corner and disappeared. Blake stood there for a moment, running the afternoon back through his mind before starting the walk back to his apartment.

Back at his apartment, he started the book Sarah had recommended, and without realizing it, he mentally noted specific parts he would tell her about the next time they saw each other. As he flipped through the pages of his book, Blake felt peace sink into his spirit a little more than it had, even earlier that day. The sun set, the stars twinkled through the dark sky above, and Blake settled deeper into his reading chair with a warm cup of tea. The story kept him company the rest of the night until he finally took a break and went to bed.

Fast asleep that night, he dreamt of cozy chairs, warm smiles, and secret libraries.

Outside, winds blow
And leaves shake
Anxiously

Inside, tomes sleep
And records sing
Pleasantly

Enchanting Forest
Full of wonder and
Peaceful quiet

What wonderful treasures
You can find
Hidden among the trees

$$- \mathcal{C.E}$$

35 mm

Jess realized she was tapping her pen too loudly at her desk, but she just couldn't help it. Her nerves were coming out in anxious spurts of energy that, unfortunately for her co-workers, manifested itself in the constant *tap, tap, tap* of her pen as the minutes slowly ticked closer to 5:00.

Jess hadn't been much of a camper for the past several years. She loved being outdoors, especially as Fall was starting to set in, but it had been a long time since she had stayed outside overnight. It'd been even longer since her and her husband, Noah, had done a trip like this without the kids. Now, though, Blake had moved off to start grad school, and Caleb was certainly old enough to stay at home by himself as he went to and from work for the weekend. So, for the first time in years, Jess and Noah were taking the weekend to themselves and going camping.

They had spent the last several days gathering their old camping gear together: a two-person tent, some dusty sleeping bags, and a lot of supplies for making a fire and cooking dinner over it. Noah assured Jess that the weather would be perfect for camping, but Jess had her doubts. She felt anxiety constructing scenarios in her head of freezing temperatures and heavy rain coming with darkness that night. She tried to push the worry to the back of her mind, but she still felt nervous.

With 45 minutes left in the work day, Jess was going over all the things they'd packed and their plan for the next day in her mind until she could've recited it in her sleep.

38 minutes left

Tap, tap, tap

37 minutes left

Tap, tap, tap

It had been a slow day at work, as it often was on Fridays. She was a manager at a tech company that was headquartered near her home, and although most of the week was packed with meetings and "collaboration sessions," Fridays often gave her a respite from the chaos as everyone wound down the week, and some even took off early for the day. She rarely took much time off, certainly not on a random Friday, so she had resigned herself to staying in the office until right at 5:00.

She sat in a conference room with a couple of her friends and fellow managers as they all wrapped up tasks and sent their final emails for the week.

30 minutes left

Tap, tap, tap

She noticed her friend, Alyssa, look up from across the conference table at the restless pen and frown.

"Sorry," Jess said and focused all her willpower on keeping the pen still. Alyssa raised an eyebrow.

"Aren't you and Noah going camping this weekend?"

"Yeah," Jess replied. "We're leaving as soon as we get home from work."

"And doesn't Noah typically get off a little earlier than you?" Alyssa continued.

"Well, yeah."

"Then what are you doing here? Go home! Go camping!"

Before Jess could protest, the other managers jumped in, echoing Alyssa, assuring her there wasn't anything else she needed to do. Jess almost insisted, but she looked at her laptop and realized the screen had gone to sleep a long time ago and sat blank with nothing but her reflection looking back at her. Yeah, she was done.

With a quick "Thanks," and "See you all later," she was packed up and out the door! Outside, there was a cool, late-September breeze that was coming in as the sun sank a little closer to the horizon. It wasn't quite golden hour, but it was heading in that direction. It was time to start the weekend.

On her way home, Jess stopped by a local coffee shop to quickly grab an iced coffee. It was her last sweet treat before heading into the wilderness! Having the window rolled down in the drive thru was nice with the cool breeze outside, and she enjoyed it so much, she kept her window down the rest of the drive home. She willed her worries from the work week to fly out of her mind and into the September air as she prepared herself to leave it all behind that weekend.

When she arrived at home, Caleb's car was already gone, indicating he had left for his job at the hardware store. Meanwhile, Jess could tell that Noah was in full-on preparation mode from how both the front door and the back door of their truck were wide open. Inside, Noah was in a whirlwind of packing and organizing their camping gear as he ran from the house to the truck and back again (a rhythm he briefly interrupted to kiss Jess hello, of course).

Jess took a minute to change out of her work clothes and sit, sipping her iced coffee, before jumping into the chaos of rolling sleeping bags and stuffing their backpacks with water bottles. She felt sure she had everything packed, but at the last second she remembered her film camera. She had discovered it in her parents' basement over the summer and had decided to clean it up to use.

Of course, she hadn't taken the time to really do much with it yet, but earlier that week she had bought film for it and committed to using it on their trip. She opened the box she had stashed it away in, and the lens flashed at her in the light, as if to say *hello!*

Carefully, she placed it in its leather case and tucked it away in her pack. With that, they had everything they needed. In their rush to leave with enough time before sundown, Jess realized how warm she had gotten and was glad to once again step out into the cooler air when they left the house for the final time and locked the door behind them.

Jess climbed into the passenger side, and Noah hopped into the driver seat and let out a deep breath. As they pulled out of the driveway, Jess turned on some properly adventurous music and rolled the window down to let the breeze in. The tizzy of packing had distracted her, but now she was relaxing again. With the moment of peace, though, came the nerves that she'd blocked out with coffee and preparation earlier.

She had always loved being outside - she had probably spent half her childhood climbing trees in her front lawn - but camping out overnight gave her pause. Maybe she'd listened to too many true crime podcasts, but the dark woods just made her nervous. As she pondered the hidden dangers that were in store for them that evening, Jess began to nod off to the movement of the truck, and eventually, the fatigue of the work week took over, and she dozed off.

She woke with a start as the truck lurched.

"Well good morning," Noah laughed, glancing sideways at her as he drove.

"Good morning," Jess mumbled back as she rubbed her eyes. "Are we there yet?"

Noah laughed again, "Not quite, but we did just hit the last stretch before the trailhead. This is the gravel road I was telling you about."

Jess could tell they'd left the paved road before he'd even said anything by the way the truck was bouncing around. She grabbed onto the handle above her seat and tried to keep steady as they rocked this way and that. There was a canopy of trees above them filtering light down to the road below, but she couldn't quite tell how much light was left. Seeing her looking up, Noah answered the unasked question,

"Yeah, it seems to be getting darker a little quicker than we had thought it would, but that's ok, the campsite isn't very far down the trail, and we should be there in about 15 minutes or so."

Jess nodded and settled back in her seat, still holding on to the handle. Just as he had said, after 15 more minutes of bumping along the road, they pulled into a small parking area. Noah parked the truck and hopped out to start unloading. Jess sat in her seat for just a moment longer as she let her impromptu nap fade more before she opened the creaky door and hopped out, herself.

The two of them wordlessly gathered their camping gear together and heaved their packs onto their backs for the hike ahead. Jess opted to take the tent in her pack so Noah would be free to carry their cooler and some of the cooking gear they'd brought. The packs were heavy, but neither of them complained as they loaded everything up.

Finally, Jess brought out the camera case from the pack she had placed it in. The slim, leather case had a strap that she carefully lowered over her head, letting the weight rest on her neck. She unclipped the top of the case, revealing the camera inside. It was an old Kodak 35mm film camera that hadn't been used much, but Jess remembered her dad bringing it out a few times when she was a teenager.

Jess didn't consider herself a photographer by any means, but she did love capturing the world in photographs when she could. Typically, she just used her phone, but the idea of *crafting* a picture on film was exciting compared to the thoughtless snaps that filled her digital camera roll. She was a bit nervous handling the vintage equipment, though, and she wasn't sure how she would decide which pictures to take. It would be a bit of a learning process.

As they approached the unmarked trailhead, Jess gingerly slid the camera out of the case and pointed it at the trees. She hovered over a leaf that had turned red and practiced putting the picture into focus and opening up the aperture of the lens to capture the light correctly. The sight focused just right and the camera itself almost seemed to hold its breath in anticipation. The lens lingered on the leaf for a moment, but Jess never took the shot. Instead, she slid the camera back into the case and promised herself she would be decisive enough to take *some* pictures on their trip. Eventually.

She looked back up at the sky and thought that the sun seemed to have sunk lower than she was comfortable with. She frowned to herself but decided against commenting on it, trusting Noah would get them to the campsite all right. She just hoped it wasn't completely dark when they got there.

The map she had looked at earlier that day had said it was a 7-mile hike to an overlook, but Jess remembered the campsite was off the trail just a couple miles in, so she was optimistic she wouldn't have to haul her pack around for too terribly long. As they began their journey, the cool breeze rustled the leaves on the trees around them in rhythm with their steps as they marched on. Normally, Jess would enjoy the peaceful atmosphere, but her anxiety kept relaxation at bay as the sun sank lower.

Ahead of her, Noah was forging ahead on the trail as the early fall leaves crunched underfoot. Every so often, Noah would slow down to stare at the woods around them. Jess followed his glances at the squirrels that hopped from branch to branch overhead and to the splashes of Autumn color that were starting to bleed through in the trees. It was all very beautiful in the golden light, but she kept her glances brief so as not to lose focus on the hike.

As Noah stopped to take in the sights, Jess had to stop herself from bumping into him. She enjoyed golden hour as much as the next person, but she was intent on beating the darkness to the campsite. She would have taken the lead, but Noah had actually hiked the trail before, and seeing the side trails that split off every hundred yards or so, Jess figured it would be easier to let Noah lead in the correct direction. That didn't stop her from feeling a little annoyed when he dragged his feet, though.

When Noah stopped to snap a picture of a tree with his phone, Jess' annoyance boiled over enough to elicit an audible sigh.

"Oh, am I holding you up?" Noah laughed looking back at her. "I would've thought you'd be taking pictures, too, on that camera. It's perfect lighting right now for it."

Jess bit back a frustrated remark. Instead, she flashed an exasperated smile, "Well, I think there will be plenty of time for pictures when we get to the campsite. You know. *Before* nightfall."

Noah put his phone back in his pocket and held up his hands in surrender, "Fair enough, I'm moving."

The two of them continued on as the shadows stretched farther on the ground around them. They continued on in silence for a while until Jess couldn't take it anymore.

"How much farther is it?"

"We're over halfway there, so it shouldn't be far now."

Jess could tell Noah was trying not to get agitated, himself, and she felt bad for a moment about being pushy. On the other hand, she could feel her nerves settling into a tight ball in her chest as she watched the sun drop below the horizon, and that made her feel justified in her pushiness. She did not want to be wandering through the woods in the dark.

Without verbalizing it, the two of them picked up their pace, knowing that there would only be another half hour or so of light left. The intensity of their footsteps increased, and the sound felt deafening as the woods grew quieter around them. Jess was aware of the fading colors and the strain her eyes felt as light withdrew from the woods around them. Too soon, they were hiking in darkness. A chill creeped into the air.

Noah paused for a moment and got out a small flashlight, assuring Jess that they were close to the campsite and that everything would be fine. Jess hardly heard him over her own beating heart. The once-peaceful forest was now home to all sorts of dangers in her mind. Snapping twigs and rustling leaves were no longer from cute squirrels bouncing through the trees but large men chasing them down in the dark. She tried to breathe deeply to calm herself down, but doing that while hiking with a 20lb backpack nearly caused her to start hyperventilating. *I thought we were nearly there!*

They continued to march down the trail, now a little slower so they didn't trip over roots they couldn't see anymore. Just as Jess was about ready to stop and set up camp in the middle of the trail, the dim flashlight Noah was holding revealed a small clearing on the path ahead, and the two of them practically sprinted towards it.

"We're here!" Noah said (a little louder than Jess would've preferred). Jess didn't have the energy to respond and just sat down, dropping her pack to the side. She looked around at their home for the night, and she was unsettled by the long shadows cast by the trees in the dim moonlight. She was anxious to get more light. Taking in the scene made her chest feel tight with nervousness, and she slipped the heavy camera case off from around her neck to breathe in deeper. *I need to calm down,* she thought to herself.

"Do you want to set up the tent or get the fire started?" Noah asked, knowing she would, in fact, have a preference.

Jess sighed quietly and stood back up. "Do you even have to ask?"

Even in the dim light, she could tell he was smiling at her response as he handed off the striker he had stuffed in his pack on the way out and began to set up the tent. In the moonlight, Jess could see that there was already a spot where some long-gone campers had created a fire pit with some large stones, so she grabbed a flashlight from her pack and marched over.

There were pieces of charred logs still in the pit, so she gathered them together and cleared out some of the leaves from around the edges. She set them aside to use for kindling later, and then she started gathering fallen branches and twigs from the tree line. Putting together the ingredients for a campfire was always comforting to Jess, and it took her mind off of the deep darkness of the woods around them.

When they were younger, before they had kids, Jess and Noah had gone camping many times, and she had always been in charge of building the fire. She loved the moment when the flames settled into the kindling and steadily grew into a full fire. The light and warmth that followed felt like a reward for the work that had gone into it. As she continued gathering sticks and placing them by the fire pit, she wondered when she had stopped feeling at home in the natural world.

By the time she was satisfied with her pile of firewood, she had worked up a light sweat. The cool, night air was feeling more refreshing than it had when the sun had first gone down. Jess carefully arranged the kindling in the center of the firepit, placing dry leaves and small twigs together in the middle of a teepee of larger branches, just like she'd been taught growing up. Once the pieces were all together, Jess got out her striker and carefully struck the pieces together to cause sparks to rain down into the center of the tinder. Warm light flashed for a second, and Jess' heart leapt at the sight.

When she was younger, it took forever for her to get a flame going, but despite not having practiced in years, it only took a few tries for the sparks to settle into the dry, crushed leaves and start to smolder. Jess threw more sparks on top of it for good measure and gently blew air once, then twice, and on the third time a small flame appeared and quickly consumed the dry leaves around it.

Seeing the flame's dim light made Jess relax a little more, and she fed it more leaves to keep it going. Soon it moved on to the twigs, and when it had overtaken them, the flames caught the slightly larger sticks. It grew until the small branches were overrun with golden light, and warmth flowed out of the circle of stones.

Jess continued to feed it more kindling and branches until she felt satisfied it would sustain itself for a while. She sat down, now conscious of the smile that had snuck its way onto her face, and watched the flames, mesmerized by the movement and the soft glow.

"All done!" Noah exclaimed behind her, interrupting her trance.

Jess tore her eyes away from the fire, still smiling, "Great! Looks like we're all set up."

Noah returned her smile as he walked over and sat next to her. Jess leaned her head on his shoulder and sighed.

"That's better."

Soon, the two of them had set up their fold-up camping chairs and were sitting by the warm fire, roasting hot dogs and s'mores. Finishing their feast, they both felt the stress of the work week melt away, and laughter overtook the night as they talked and told stories they both already knew but loved to hear anyway. Jess felt the clearing transform into a bright, cozy home for them to dwell in for the evening.

In fact, looking around she saw how the golden light from the fire blended with the silver moonlight to bathe the trees around them in an incredible glow. The once-creepy woods was now an enchanting forest full of life and beauty. She breathed in deep and smelled the scent of the fire mixing with the pine needles on the trees and scattered on the ground. Jess caught Noah staring at her as she gaped and took it all in, and she blushed in spite of herself. He smiled and silently gestured to her camera case where she had left it by her pack.

Jess' eyes lit up, and she quickly retrieved it. The camera sat expectantly in its case, waiting to be put to use. She slid it out and began adjusting the settings to let more light in through the lens and keep the shutter open longer on the shot, since it was dark. When she felt like she had the best low-light settings possible, she aimed the camera at the campfire where Noah was sitting. He looked up and smiled big.

Click

She lingered on the shot, taking in the scene of her husband sitting by the warm fire. The tightness in her chest had almost fully loosened now, and the joy of being outside, away from screens and emails was setting in. She focused on the tent Noah had constructed that was lit up by the fire.

Click

She zoomed in on the glowing leaves that were tinged red and orange on the trees nearby.

Click

Jess captured as much of the night as she could without running through her film roll, and Noah insisted on taking a few with her in it, of course. Soon though, she stopped so she could take more in the morning with the remaining exposures. She was already excited to see how the photos turned out, even if she didn't end up having the settings quite right.

She was finding the practice of making all those little adjustments and waiting to see the result felt, well, fun. There was something about it that felt so *real*. Out of habit, Jess was tempted to pull out her phone to capture the moments digitally, too, but she decided against it. That night would only live in their memories and on film.

The night stretched on, and they let the fire die out on its own. When it finally disappeared in smoldering ash, Jess was stunned at how many stars they could see, even with the moon out. Living in the city, she'd almost forgotten how vast the night sky looked. It was terrifying in the most exciting way. It wasn't long before their bodies relaxed into drowsiness, and they crawled into the tent to give into their exhaustion and fall asleep.

The next morning, Jess woke up naturally as the sun was rising in the sky. She could hear the birds chirping outside the tent, and a gentle breeze was rustling the leaves on the trees above. Jess' joints felt stiff as she sat up in her sleeping bag - she was used to a much softer mattress, after all - but she was content.

Noah was already up, and Jess heard him moving around outside the tent. She poked her head out of the tent flap and saw that he had a fire going (even though that was her job!) and was making breakfast. He noticed her peeking out and smiled.

"Breakfast is served!"

Jess grinned wide and crawled out of the tent, stretching hard as she stood up.

"My hero!"

The two of them sat in their camping chairs and scarfed down bacon and campfire pancakes that Noah had cooked in an old pan. It was the best meal they had eaten in what felt like months. For the next hour or so they sat by the fire, taking in the beautiful day that was coming alive. They each read books that they had stashed in their packs, gently holding hands until they had to turn a page. Jess already felt like a new person.

Unfortunately, they had to go back by the afternoon, so as lunch time approached, they went ahead and packed up most of their gear, including the tent. They left out stuff for sandwiches and ate quickly so they could take their time on the hike back. Neither of them was interested in rushing the day, if possible.

They loaded everything up, packs full and camera situated comfortably around Jess' neck, and they began their stroll back down the trail they came from. This time, they had a clearer idea of how long it would be to the trailhead, though they were paying much less attention to the time now. In fact, as they began their hike, Jess realized she hadn't looked at her phone all morning. She'd just been relying on Noah's simple wristwatch to tell the time. That felt rather freeing.

Their return journey felt lighter and more joyful to Jess than the one the night before, and they stopped frequently to inspect an interesting tree or admire the autumn colors that were setting in. Now readjusting her camera's settings for daylight, Jess captured the forest around them liberally.

Click

A shot of the canopy of leaves above them.

Click

A photo of Noah on the trail smiling back at her.

Click

A squirrel that posed on a tree branch.

Click

Finally, Jess was focusing the lens on a vine that was growing beside the path, thinking the orange-yellow flowers on it seemed familiar, when she realized she had already used the last exposure on her roll of film. She smiled to herself, remembering how worried she'd been that she wouldn't take enough photos. She couldn't wait to see them developed.

A week or so later, back in reality, she stopped at the local photography shop on her way home from work to pick up her developed pictures. When she got back to the house, she and Noah flipped through the prints together, recalling their adventure in grand detail, promising they would do it again soon.

Work was still stressful, and life was still loud and overwhelming when they got back, but Jess felt lighter thinking about their experience of being reintroduced to life away from the noise, and she found it easier to put away all of the things that fought for her attention and focus on capturing photos on her new/old camera.

In their backyard, Jess often found herself over the next several weeks watching birds lightly drift into the branches of a tree and sit among the now scarlet and gold leaves.

She'd carefully point the lens at the bird, focus the image, adjust the aperture, and-
Click!

Comfortable light
Cool breeze
Vibrant color
All around

Deep breaths in
And out
Delicious food that
Nourishes and relaxes

Cleansing detachment from
Worries that weigh us
Down and leave us feeling
Cold and digital

Careful and gentle
Adjustments that
Bring life into
Warm focus

Click!

- *C.E.*

Walk in the Forest

Over the years I've become quite familiar with the Forest, and I have shared these Autumn Tales with many others who have wandered in, but I wasn't always so at home here. My journey has been full of difficulties like anyone else, and it took a few wrong turns and mishaps before I found my way to where I am now.

On a day very much like today, I also found myself wandering among the trees, much like our friends in these stories, and maybe like you are now. It was a chilly afternoon with gray clouds hanging over the trees. They covered the world like a great, big blanket, but instead of keeping warmth in, it made everything cooler. The trees were all nearly bare, with just a handful of leaves clinging desperately to the branches as the wind blew through. The dead leaves on the ground crunched loudly as I walked.

It was eerily quiet as I walked between the trees. Aside from the leaves underfoot, there wasn't a sound to be heard. Once or twice, I stepped on a stray branch on the ground and the sound of it cracking was so loud in the silence that it startled me.

Despite the ominous feeling in the air, I was excited about exploring. It was a deep, vast wood, and I just knew there were all sorts of interesting things to find. For what felt like hours, I wove between trees, crunching leaves and snapping branches underfoot as I went. A couple times I came across a squirrel or a bird that was racing through the trees, and they would quickly veer away from where I was when they noticed me.

At one point, I had come to the foot of a rather large hill and decided to climb up and over it. The climb started off easily enough, but the higher I went, the steeper the hill seemed to become, and soon, my old hiking boots were slipping on the layer of leaves that covered the ground beneath my feet. Several times I had to catch myself on the small trees that sprouted out of the hillside. Eventually, I was almost entirely using the trees to pull myself up the hill.

I thought I was nearing the top of the hill, finally, when a particularly brittle branch that I'd grabbed onto snapped in my hand and sent me tumbling down the hill. I rolled and rolled, picking up dead leaves as I went, until I landed at the foot of a large oak tree. I was disoriented and frustrated but not injured in any major way.

Grumbling a little, I got up and brushed away the dirt and leaves that were stuck to my sweatshirt and in my hair. With renewed determination, I marched up the hill again. This time I was more careful of which branches I used as handholds.

I had begun to question if I had found a small mountain instead of a hill when I finally found the summit of my personal Everest. I hauled myself to the flat area on top and laid down to catch my breath. I sank into the lush carpet of leaves and watched the gray clouds shift in the wind above. I could tell the sunlight that was filtering through the clouds was beginning to fade, and I became very aware that I was far from any form of shelter or safety. I cut my break short and jumped to my feet. It was time to move on.

As I brushed myself off again, I took in my surroundings, and through the trees I saw a small creek. I walked in the direction of the stream and could hear it gurgling as I got closer. I knew I needed to get across, but it was just deep enough and wide enough that I hesitated, not wanting to completely soak my feet wading through. *If only there was a bridge or even a large log to walk across on.* My thoughts were answered by something catching my eye downstream to my right.

Not too far, there was what looked like a tree that had fallen across the creek. It seemed like a large tree, hopefully wide enough to walk across without too much difficulty. I walked towards it cautiously, trying to examine it for any sign of defect or structural issues. Falling fully into the icy water that was rushing beside me sounded like an easy way to ruin an afternoon. Getting closer, I realized it was not a fallen tree at all. It was, in fact, a giant root that had apparently grown up and across the creek! I couldn't believe it!

The strange root sprouted from a large, old tree on the other side that was swaying in the breeze as if it were inviting me across. I eyed it skeptically, weighing my options and debating its ability to support me as I crossed.

Just then, as I approached the natural bridge, I saw something scurry across it. A rabbit had apparently been sitting on it, camouflaged against its soft brown exterior, and when I got closer, it darted across the root to the other side and into the thick foliage. I decided if it was good enough for the locals, it was good enough for me.

Excited, but cautious, I approached the large root and, step by step, walked over. From above, the once-small creek now looked like a roaring river that would sweep me away if I had the bad luck of falling in. The subtle spray of what that I felt leaping up to my face was ice cold, and I could see that it had covered the root in a slick layer of water.

As I slowly made my way across, I distributed my weight carefully so I wouldn't fall if I slipped, which I eventually did once or twice. Without too much drama, I finally found myself on the other side and hopped off.

I took in my new surroundings and saw there was a faint path that wound between the trees, but it wasn't particularly obvious. I attempted to follow the path as I pressed onwards and through the wood. In the distance, there were sounds of creatures moving in the shadows behind trees, and I felt a shiver run through me. I hoped this wasn't a place where bears lived.

Occasionally I would catch a flash of movement in my peripheral and whip my head around to catch a glimpse of brown or gray dashing behind a tree. Hoping my company was friendly, I continued.

Several times I got distracted by the trees towering up around me and lost the path, forcing myself to double back to find it again. After following it for a while, it took a sharp turn and split on either side of a tree. It was a pine tree that seemed unnaturally large. Most of the trees in the forest weren't small by any means, but this one was noticeably wider. At a glance, it seemed like the trunk would've taken at least four or five people to wrap all the way around it. I figured it would be taller, too, than most trees in the forest if I could have seen up high enough through the branches.

Not wanting to leave it to conjecture, I leapt up to the lowest branch I could find and began hauling myself up the trunk, going from branch to branch. Many of the branches were large enough for me to stand on without fear of breaking them, but there were plenty of smaller ones that I could grab onto for support.

I climbed and climbed, racing faster and faster as I felt more confident in my abilities. The pine bark scraped my hands as I went, but I hardly cared about that. Through the pine needles and branches, I could see an incredible view stretching out as I went higher. The branches were starting to get thinner and sparser, forcing me to slow down, and I came to a stop on the last branch I could find to support my weight.

I settled onto the branch and took in the expanse of treetops I saw before me. A flood of orange and red spread out in every direction, and the sun drenched every leaf in soft gold. The cool air blew the leaves together and the sound was nearly deafening from up there. In the distance, I could see mountains rising up in dark blue shadows. It was a perfect moment of calm after the tense journey I'd made so far.

Just as I was thinking I could stare at the scene forever, the sun sank behind a mountaintop and the world began to fade into darkness.

October

Into the Maiz

It had been a slow day that was full of studying for the tests Hannah had coming up the following week. That's how a lot of Saturdays had turned out to be in college. August and September had flown by in a blur of papers, tests, and reintroducing herself to everyone she interacted with. October began slower, but the classwork was still unending. It wasn't until a phone call with her mom that Hannah decided she needed to get out of her room more.

During her first two months of college, she had become very familiar with her dorm and the routine of staying in to study and watch her favorite TV show. It didn't even occur to her that this was abnormal, she just needed space to crack down on her studies. Listening to her mom talk about their move and her little brother, Ben, on the phone, she felt a pang of nostalgia for the adventures of home.

With Hannah going away to college and Lucy also moving off for her new job, Hannah could tell things were different for her parents and Ben. She thought back to just last Fall when she was a Senior in high school, alternating every night spending time with friends and her family as they visited pumpkin patches, decorated the house with reds and oranges, and played all sorts of games together while the world outside cooled to a temperature fit for Autumn.

Now Fall was in full swing, and Hannah was painfully aware of how different life was so far in college and the ever-increasing anxiety about not having friends there to do any of those things with. It was hard enough to be away from her siblings, but being around so many people who were basically strangers still felt really lonely.

Even with her roommate, Samantha, things had not been as easy as she thought it'd be. Instead of the built-in best friend she'd expected, Samantha was more of an acquaintance that Hannah spoke with in brief sentences in the rare moments she was actually in the dorm and didn't have her headphones on. Hannah had no idea what she was listening to, and Samantha didn't share. Regardless, she didn't seem very open to new friends.

Hannah didn't have the heart to bring up Autumn while on the phone, knowing her mom had likely already filled their new house to the brim with plastic pumpkins and Fall candles. To say Hannah's dorm paled in comparison to this image would've been an understatement.

That week, after thinking about last Fall's adventures, Hannah finally decided to put herself out there and try to make some new friends. She thought she might even try to get a group together to watch a scary movie or two. Being a freshman, there was no shortage of girls her age who were extremely enthusiastic about Fall activities. It wasn't long before a group of friends that were in her biology class invited her to come along on their trip to a local pumpkin patch that weekend.

Now Hannah was pacing her dorm room, waiting for the group of, essentially, strangers to pick her up. She did and redid her hair several times but eventually settled on a simple ponytail and put on a flannel shirt and her work boots, the kind she didn't mind getting a little muddy.

This was normally the kind of night that made Fall feel magical, but some of that magic was lost this time because of the nervousness that was clouding Hannah's mind. It had been a long time since she'd had to make new friends, and she was nervous about spending time with new people. She would've invited Samantha to come along, but she was nowhere to be found when Hannah returned from class, so she waited in her dorm alone.

The girls were supposed to pick Hannah up around 5:00, so she made her way downstairs to the dorm lobby 10 minutes early. She sat and waited, checking her phone off and on, trying to push down her anxious feelings. *4:53.*

She started off on a small couch in the lobby, but feeling jittery, she got up and paced the tile floor. *4:56.*

She glanced outside, nervous to miss them by accident, and, eventually, she pushed through the doors and sat on the steps outside, overlooking the parking lot. *4:59.*

She checked and rechecked her phone just to make sure she hadn't missed a call or text from someone. The cool breeze reminded her of the jacket she had left in the room. She couldn't bring herself to abandon her post, though. *5:04.*

She bounced her leg up and down anxiously. *Where were they?*

Just then, a blue Jeep pulled into the parking lot and rolled up to the curb by the stairs. A quick glance confirmed the girls she was waiting on were piled inside. Hannah couldn't quite tell which seat was free through the tinted windows, but Brittany, who was in the passenger seat, pointed to the seat behind her, so Hannah hopped in, trying to be nonchalant, of course. Quick pleasantries were exchanged, and the Jeep was off to the corn maze.

On the drive, Hannah didn't say a whole lot. Between the loud music (most of which was unfamiliar to her) and inside jokes that only the other three had context for, there wasn't much room to get a word in. This did not help the worry that was sitting on her chest about the friendships she felt were on the line tonight. Hannah distracted herself by gazing out the window as they passed golden wheat fields and pine trees. She tried to avoid it, but her thoughts drifted to nights spent at corn mazes with her family and friends back home. She hoped tonight would live up to her nostalgia.

At the farm, they quickly got in line to get their entry tickets, and Hannah could feel her nose get a little itchy. Hay seemed to cover every inch of the barn the ticket counter was in, and her allergies were fully aware of it. The familiar sensation was oddly comforting - some things never change. Once through the line, their group immediately moved towards the corn maze to see if they could find their way through the twisting paths.

The farm was bustling with activity that evening. Families were rushing past with their kids, going to the concession stands or the petting zoo, teenagers were riding the small zip line, and what looked like a few youth groups from local churches were scattered among various activity stations. Hannah was surprised at how big the place was considering the humble barn they entered through.

The girls walked with purpose to the start of the corn maze, flashed the wristbands to the worker standing nearby, and walked through the entrance marked with a sign that said "Adults (Difficult)." Hannah was never the best at mazes, so she hoped the others were. Inside, the golden stalks towered over their heads and surrounded them on all sides.

They marched down the path, and it wasn't long before they came to a fork that went off in different directions. The four of them paused, looking back and forth between the two, pondering which seemed better.

"Ready everyone?" Brittany asked the group. Before anyone answered she took off into the corn maze to the right and disappeared around the next corner. Kathryn also took off, this time to the left, sprinting out of sight.

Crystal started to follow, but hesitated, "Oh, I don't know if we mentioned before, but we always race to see who can finish the corn maze first. Is that alright?"

"Of course," Hannah said automatically, "I'll see you at the end."

Crystal lingered a beat before taking off down a path, herself, leaving Hannah alone. She sighed quietly to herself and started walking. She had hoped the corn maze would be a chance to get to know the group better, but it didn't seem like that was going to happen. Hannah wandered down the path, choosing turns to take at random. The cornstalks surrounded her on all sides, now, and she was lost in the maze. As she walked, she listened for signs that anyone else was around, but all she heard was the breeze rustling the leaves.

The sun sank lower as she walked, and soon, the shadows from the tall stalks had grown to nearly cover the entire path. Hannah attempted to walk in the small patch of light, avoiding the chilly shadows, but that was becoming harder by the minute. Somewhere, she a crow called out, and she jumped at the interruption to the silence. Aside from the birds, though, Hannah was all alone in her section of the maze.

So much for being besties, she thought to herself, wondering if the others had already found the exit.

With the sun setting quickly, Hannah became agitated at each turn as she hit dead end after dead end. Finally, she decided to cut through the walls of corn and try to catch up with the others when she got out.

She pushed into the golden-brown wall in front of her and started jogging, swiping at the leaves in front of her face. Not seeing the outside, she picked up her pace and jogged faster until a crow, hidden in the corn, cawed loudly nearby and startled her, again, causing her to jump and land her foot on a stray corn cob. Hannah stumbled and fell hard through the stalks around her. Grumbling, she pushed herself to her feet, brushing off mud that had gotten on her jeans, and she realized she had stumbled into a small clearing.

The sky was getting darker, but the clearing allowed the last bit of light to peek into the field in that spot, and Hannah could see a tall plant sprouting up in the middle of the area. She looked closer and saw that it was a group of sunflowers, almost as tall as the corn around her. The bright yellow petals stood out and shook happily in the breeze.

"Whoa!" Hannah heard behind her, "Where did those come from?"

She turned and saw Crystal pushing through the corn and into the clearing.

"I don't know," Hannah responded, grateful for the coincidental timing. "Maybe they were planted here?"

"That's an odd place to plant sunflowers." Crystal said. "Though, I supposed it's even more of an odd place for them to pop up naturally."

The two of them sat silently for a beat, taking in the bright flowers as the last rays of sunlight caught the petals.

"How did you get here?" Hannah asked, breaking the silence.

Without taking her eyes off the flowers, Crystal answered, "Eh, I got lost and was tired of trying to find the exit. I almost always end up cutting through the walls, anyway."

At that, Hannah smiled, "Yeah, me too."

Suddenly there was a rustling on the other side of the clearing, and out from the corn came Brittany and Kathryn.

"Well, look who it is," Crystal said, "You're late to the party!"

The others laughed and explained that they had run into each other and had also gotten tired of trying to find the exit. Hannah laughed with them about their collectively poor navigation skills.

"Quick!" Crystal said, "Before the light is gone!"

She pulled out her phone and corralled the four of them into position in front of the sunflowers for a selfie. Seeing the image on the screen, Hannah couldn't help but smile big at the four of them with the bright flowers and sunset sky in the background. They individually took pictures with the flowers, too, before plotting a course to get out of there, now together. Hannah was relieved to not have to get out of the maze by herself. Before they left the clearing, Crystal stopped Hannah and broke off one of the smaller flowers.

"Here," she said, tucking it into the shirt pocket of Hannah's flannel, "As the one who discovered the secret garden, it's only right you should have something to show for it."

Blushing slightly at the kind gesture, Hannah told her thank you - nonchalantly, of course - and they started pushing back through the corn in the direction they thought might be the most likely to get them out of there.

Soon, they had made their way back into the open air of the farm and found themselves on the side of the maze where the pumpkin patch sat for people to search through for their Fall decor. Several families were sifting through the green vines, now using phone flashlights to evaluate each pumpkin they came across, and the four girls joined them in wading through the plants. One by one they searched through the pumpkins, looking for the perfect ones for their dorm rooms, when, finally, they all had found the right pumpkin for each of them.

The one Hannah had grabbed was a medium-sized, perfect sphere that had a long, curly stem growing out from the top. The color was a rich orange that practically shouted out at her from the greenery it sat in. She couldn't wait to carve into it! She imagined triangular eyes and a wicked smile stretching across the front of it and felt content with her choice. Now satisfied with their finds, the girls were all starting to shiver from the cool of the night setting in.

Fortunately, there was a hot chocolate stand, so they set their pumpkins by a few chairs nearby, and paid a few dollars each at the stand for four cups of warmth. They grabbed them quickly and held them tight, not taking a sip yet, just letting it warm their exposed hands. They settled into the chairs sat by the fire one of the workers had just kindled in the small fire pit.

As the fire warmed them up more, they sipped their hot chocolates and let it warm their insides as well. They spent the next half hour laughing, telling stories, and taking poorly-lit pictures by that fire. Hannah was already sure she would remember the experience for a long time. Looking up to the sky, she saw that a harvest moon had risen that kind of resembled the bright orange pumpkin she had picked. She felt content with her autumn evening.

As the soft light faded with the flames, Crystal subtly suggested they needed to get back to campus soon, and checking the time, they all agreed. When they finally got in the car to head back, Hannah found herself admiring the sunflower tucked into her shirt pocket.

The nervousness she had started the evening with had faded with the sunlight, and she felt more at home than she had before. Not quite ready for the night to end, she went out on a limb and suggested going back and playing games, which they enthusiastically agreed to!

They went back to Kathryn's dorm, where they stayed well into the night, loudly laughing and swapping stories from high school. By the time she left, Hannah could hardly remember what she'd been nervous about earlier. Before they finally separated for the evening, Kathryn made a point to add everyone to a group chat so they could find a time to carve their pumpkins, and Hannah practically cheered! Being away from home was difficult at times like this, but she was already starting to feel better.

When Hannah returned to the dorm, Samantha was back and folding laundry. She jumped when the door closed, slightly jostling her headphones. She pulled them the rest of the way off.

"There you are. You're almost never out this late."

So, you do notice, Hannah thought to herself, and she explained where she'd been.

"Oh," Samantha responded. "That sounds like fun. Wow, I haven't done that in a long time."

Hannah paused, trying to decide her next words carefully.

"Well, there's plenty of time left in the season, and I'd love to go again if you want." She placed her pumpkin on her chest of drawers as she spoke. "We could get you a matching one and carve them sometime."

Samantha fiddled with her headphones for a second, but after a beat said, "Y-yeah, that sounds fun." Then she retreated back into her music and continued folding her laundry.

Well, it's a start, Hannah thought. *Maybe we'll be friends after all.*

Just then, Kathryn texted the group message, *Tonight was so fun! I'm glad we got to hang out! Goodnight everyone!*

Crystal responded with one of the pictures she'd taken of the four of them by the sunflowers.

Yes, it was sooo fun! What a beautiful night!

Hannah saved the picture and smiled to herself. She couldn't have agreed more.

Miniature suns
Patiently awaiting
Some wandering soul
To find them

Smiling brightly
In the Autumn sun
Welcoming friends
To come together

Quiet beauty
Secret joy
Waving goodbye
In the cool breeze

- *C.E.*

Triangle Eyes and a Wicked Smile

Lucy hadn't carved a pumpkin in years. Her friends were in college were never big on pumpkins, so neither was she, despite having done it every year growing up. Sitting in her apartment, she looked at the orange sphere leaning against the wall and tried to imagine a face on it. She frowned, thinking that she was never really the creative one in the family.

She glanced at the clock for what felt like the millionth time to find that only two minutes had passed since she had checked it last. With 30 minutes to spare after getting home from work, she found herself with an awkward amount of time to kill before she needed to leave for pumpkin carving that evening.

A couple weeks ago she had been approached by her friends at church and asked if she wanted to join for the Halloween activity. She was not particularly inclined to spend an evening washing and rewashing slimy, orange pumpkin guts off her hands, but she accepted the invitation, wanting to spend more time with her friends. Lucy hadn't been in the area for very long now since starting her new position at work, and she was grateful for any sort of social activity she could find.

Overall, she had like living in the town of "Seattle" (no, not *that* Seattle), but it had been hard finding her place in the new community. First of all, she seemed to be the only one frustrated that it shared a name with a major city. She had already had to clarify where she was now living to dozens of people from back home, and each time exasperated her a little more. Maybe she'd petition to get the name changed. That would definitely be something to do in her free time. *First pumpkin carving, then local politics.*

For now, as she was sitting on her new couch, Lucy stared at the bare walls that surrounded her. The missing wall decorations were still packed in boxes in her guest room. She thought about what her mom would say at the empty, gray walls, and smiled a little, knowing her mom couldn't stand to leave a home undecorated. Growing up, if the space didn't aggressively tell visitors what season it was, it hardly counted as home.

Lucy normally was on-board with the seasonal routine, but this year, the move had thrown her routine into a little bit of chaos, so she sat in a blank room with a blank-faced pumpkin, trying to figure out how she could stir up her creative juices to carve the pumpkin when she couldn't even hang a picture on the wall after 6 weeks of living there.

Not that moving was a great excuse, she thought to herself. *Mom and Dad moved recently, too, and I'm sure their house looks like the Fall aisle of a Hobby Lobby.* Thinking this, she felt a slight pang run through her as she realized she hadn't been back to visit in a while and really didn't know what their new home looked like now. Her imagination conjured images of what the house might look like.

She imagined her little brother, Ben, helping put up fall leaves and carve their own pumpkins. He always did a good job carving for a kid. Lucy frowned thinking about her family celebrating Fall without her. She imagined that even Hannah, although she had also moved away, would be fully into Fall festivities with her new college friends by now. She missed her family but tried to push the feelings away for now, taking comfort knowing that she'd see them for Thanksgiving in November.

In the meantime, *what was she going to do with this pumpkin?*

The bright sphere almost felt like it was shaming the dull gray walls of her apartment around it. What design could go on that face? Better yet, what design could she feasibly carve? She glanced back at the clock and was glad to see that a whole 10 minutes had passed while her thoughts wandered.

Time passed entirely too slowly when waiting to leave for an event. She decided to spend the next ten minutes looking up design inspiration on her phone, but before she found one she liked, she saw that it was time for her to leave. She hoped her timing would put her there late enough to not be the first one to arrive but early enough to not be the last either. This was an important balance to strike for a newcomer to a group, of course.

As she drove, Lucy caught the last few minutes of the red-orange sunset as it faded. The trees along the road darkened with the sky until they were menacing-looking silhouettes towering over the car as it passed by. Lucy turned the heat on low as the chill set in with the darkness. Fortunately, she had brought a light jacket, but she hoped they'd be inside for most of the evening. Then again, she really didn't know what all they were doing that night.

In the month and a half since she moved there, she'd gotten to know the people at church pretty well, but it was a struggle to build a relationship outside of weekly services. Moving a friendship into the sacred space of a home felt like an intimidating step, and Lucy wasn't sure if it'd go well. Fortunately, there would be several others joining the group that night. She just hoped she wasn't the only one dealing with a mental block on her creativity.

She pulled up to the address she'd been sent and was disappointed to see that only one other car was parked there. She waited a minute or two, pretending to be doing something on her phone, waiting for someone else to pull up, but when no one else did, she took a breath and got out of her car, grabbing the pumpkin that had sat patiently on the floor next to her.

She meandered her way to the front door and knocked. As she did, she noticed the doorbell and kicked herself for not checking for it first. Now too late, she committed to the knock, which was quickly answered by her friend, Amanda, who ushered her into the living room.

"Don't take your shoes off yet!" Amanda shouted back as she walked into the kitchen, "We'll be going outside when everyone gets here!"

I knew I should've worn a heavier jacket, Lucy thought to herself, but she just smiled at Amanda and sat on the couch. Over the next several minutes, everyone else trickled in with their pumpkins, and soon the room was filled with the dull roar of people talking and laughing with each other. Lucy found herself talking with someone named Jace who she hadn't talked much with since she moved there. He rambled on about his job in Marketing for a while before asking Lucy about her own job. As she was starting to explain what she did, Amanda got everyone's attention and led them outside to where she said they'd be carving pumpkins.

Everyone walked out and down the back steps into the backyard, following Amanda as she approached the tree line that stretched out in both directions.

"This way!" She shouted over her shoulder, disappearing into a gap in the trees.

The group moved together into the dark and found the trail Amanda was walking on. For a few minutes, all they could see was the small light from Amanda's phone up ahead, but as they turned a corner, they saw a warm glow through the trees. Amanda's phone led everyone towards the glow, and soon, they emerged into a small clearing with a bonfire roaring in the middle. Lucy blinked hard as her eyes adjusted to the light and took in the scene around her.

The fire was in a large fire pit in the center of the clearing, tended by Amanda's husband (was his name Paul, maybe?). Above, the area was further lit up by string lights that were draped across the clearing, attached to the trees. Lucy followed the lights, trying to find what powered them, and traced the strand to a small generator that was rumbling away softly just outside the edge of the clearing. Around the fire, there were several picnic tables with plastic cloths and carving tools set on top. It was perfect.

As the others took in the scene, there was a dull murmur of admiration directed towards Amanda and her husband for the setup, and Paul seemed to blush a little when Amanda channeled the compliments to him for putting the space together. Eager to put their pumpkins down, everyone quickly found a spot at one of the tables. Lucy got a spot at one of the tables that were closer to the fire, hoping the warmth would make up for the thin jacket she had on.

Amanda and Paul joined her, as did Jace. Lucy worried Jace was paying her a little too much attention, but he quickly engrossed himself in sketching out a design on his pumpkin and didn't pay her much attention. Lucy relaxed and zeroed in on her own gourd. The blank face stared at her expectantly. She picked up a marker and started to draw out her design when Amanda said something suddenly, causing her marker to slip.

"Ooh, sorry about that," Amanda said, wincing.

Lucy just laughed and wiped the errant mark away with her thumb, "No big deal. What did you say?"

"Oh, I just asked how you ended up moving here, again?"

Lucy was drawing on the pumpkin again, attempting to do two things at once. As she finished the line she was on, she responded, saying, "Work." She continued with the next line, "I work for a travel agency, and they're opening a new office in town. They asked me if I would be interested in moving to help get it started, and I thought it sounded like a fun adventure. Though this wasn't exactly what I pictured when they asked me to move to 'Seattle'"

The three of them glanced up from their pumpkins and all responded with different versions of "oh wow," as they continued on with their own designs. Lucy noted the lack of response to her Seattle joke and quickly moved on. She returned the question by asking them all about what they did, saying she had already heard about Jace's job, of course. The conversation continued like this as the four of them finished their drawings and started carving. Amanda had set out large, aluminum pans for them to throw their seeds in, and soon, the clearing was full of the sound of laughter as people plopped their seeds in by the handful.

Lucy did not like the texture of the pumpkin guts, so she used a scoop to scrape off the stringy insides. She had successfully scraped the sides clean and was about to collect the seeds at the bottom when something stopped her. She set the scoop down and tilted the pumpkin into the light to check if her eyes were playing tricks on her. One of the seeds inside had sprouted! She looked closer at the small, green sprout bursting out of the small seed. She carefully lifted it out of the hole in the top and showed it to the table.

"Have you all ever seen something like this?"

Amanda tilted her head slightly, "Hm, no, but my younger brother said he found one like that last year. I think it can happen with pumpkins if they sit for a while before they're carved."

"Huh," Lucy blinked, "I figured they had to be planted in soil to grow."

"Well, I guess it's not so much the specific place as the environment that is important," Paul piped up. "Looks like that pumpkin had just the right conditions for the little guy to start sprouting."

Amanda smiled big, "That's so cool to find!"

Lucy agreed and stared at the small sprout, pondering what to do with it. If she was back home, her younger brother, Ben, would be having a field day planning out his own personal pumpkin patch. Seeing as how she wasn't home, though, she explained to the others that she lived in an apartment and didn't have a great place to plant it.

"Here, we can take it," Amanda said, holding out her hand, "We have a small greenhouse that we grow all sorts of things in. Once it's grown we'll give it back, but in the meantime we can take care of it for you."

Lucy was taken aback by how genuine Amanda was. She carefully reached into the pumpkin, pulled out the small sprout, and handed it over. Amanda put it to the side until they had a chance to run it over to the greenhouse. Lucy was confident that under their care, a healthy pumpkin would grow from that small seed.

Noticing that everyone was wrapping up their carvings, Amanda announced to the group that her and Paul, along with a few others, would be going around and picking the top three pumpkin designs and that there would be prizes! Everyone got excited, and Lucy couldn't help but smile, thinking how much people like a friendly competition, even now in adulthood. Amanda also announced that there were things to make s'mores in a basket that everyone could get from, so several people left their masterpieces on the tables to roast marshmallows.

While waiting for a roasting stick to become available, Lucy wandered between the tables, looking at the jack-o-lanterns that people had created. She tried to guess which ones would be chosen as the best one. There was a dog, a superhero, a ghost, and even a rat (she appreciated the originality for that one). She felt a little self-conscious about her own jack-o-lantern, but she hadn't thought she would win, anyway. Besides, she wasn't the only one that went with a more subtle design. When she got the chance to grab a roasting stick, she claimed a spot by the fire to char the outside of the marshmallow that she'd use for her s'more.

By this point of the night, she found that conversation flowed much easier with those around her as they talked about what they carved and how they enjoyed Fall. Lucy got criticized, playfully, for burning her marshmallow, and she responded with a speech about how it was the only real way to eat a s'more. Her new friends laughed and rolled their eyes like they'd known each other for years. The warm fire made everything especially cozy, and Lucy was infinitely more at ease, now, than she had been when she first pulled up.

Soon, Amanda and Paul got up on one of the picnic tables to announce the winners of the carving contest. They thanked everyone for their submissions and rattled off a few honorable mentions, including Lucy's. Then they gave third and second place prizes - a flower design and cozy-looking ghost - before asking for a drumroll, and everyone started banging on the tables until they announced Jace as the winner! His Scooby-Doo design was very detailed, and Lucy was sure to snap a picture of it to send to her mom. Ben would love that!

Everyone congratulated Jace in turn, and soon, they all went back to talking and roasting s'mores. Lucy settled into a chair by the fire now, finishing off her s'more and staring at the stars that hung above them through the trees. At one point Jace came by and talked with her for a minute, complimenting her pumpkin for her "classic design." At first she thought he was making fun of her for the simple direction she went in but decided to take the comment at face value and thank him for it.

As the night went on, she talked with a few others, and they all had similar comments, saying the design was a classic for a reason. It was a small thing, but Lucy did appreciate the comments, regardless of whether or not they were completely sincere. It seemed like no matter how impressive the design actually was, this group didn't overlook a chance to encourage the newcomer. As the night was winding down, Lucy actually felt a small sense of pride in her jack-o-lantern, even if it wasn't prize-worthy. It wasn't her most creative endeavor, but it was more than she'd done in a long time.

One by one everyone started to leave, realizing how late it was, and the group dwindled to just Amanda, Paul, and Lucy, so she grabbed her pumpkin, thanked them, again, for everything, and climbed back in her car to go home.

When she got home, Lucy proudly placed her jack-o-lantern by the fireplace, this time as an accent to the room rather than a mocking presence. It was getting late, but she decided to take a minute and dig out a few of her fall decorations - a pumpkin light, some strings of leaves, a candle or two - and place them around her living room. It was subtle, but it was a start.

She lit the candle, and it trickled a cinnamon scent into the room as she turned on some music to accompany the evening.

As she officially wound down for the evening, she sank onto her sofa and looked over at her jack-o-lantern. It had triangle eyes that glowed yellow from the small candle she placed inside it and was watching her silently.

Seeing it now, Lucy laughed to herself, realizing the wicked smile she'd carved actually turned out looking happier than she'd expected.

Triangle eyes and a wicked smile
Stare, mocking from the corner

They critique and laugh
Watching for the next mistake

Triangle eyes and a wicked smile
Watch silently over the living room

When people gather and
conversation flows
The orange glow is a
quiet witness
to new friends

Triangle eyes and a wicked smile
Sit patiently in the house alone
They wait quietly
And warmly welcome the traveler home

– C.E.

An Unexpected Haunt

Ben wasn't scared of ghosts. Of course he wasn't! That's what he told anyone who would listen.

"Halloween is just for fun," he'd say, "because I'm not worried about ghosts!"

He reconfirmed this sentiment on the way to the Ghost Stories Night that was being hosted at his school on a cool October evening, just a week before Halloween. His mom had asked him if he was feeling nervous about the spooky stories, and he very quickly and very confidently assured her that he wasn't worried at all. She chuckled and told him he was very brave for his age.

Ben was now in the fourth grade, and he felt like he had a lot to prove. He was the second youngest of all his cousins (still older than his younger cousin, Bailey, though), and he was always determined not to be overlooked in the family lineup. In the Fall, that meant declaring his complete lack of fear of ghosts, ghouls, and anything else that says, "Boo!" He was especially sure to say this to his older sister, Hannah, who always talked about how spooky Halloween was. Ben never could tell if she was joking, but just in case she wasn't, he made sure to show her how brave he was.

Naturally, then, Ben had no problem going to listen to some spooky ghost stories at school before Halloween. They're just stories, after all. He and his mom arrived at the school right on time, and Ben hopped out of the car, ready to hang out with his friends. He nearly sprinted to the front doors, but his mom called out to him before he got far.

"Aren't you forgetting something?"

Ben sighed and turned back to retrieve his jacket that his mom insisted he wear when it was chilly out (though, he didn't think it was very cold at all). She helped him pull it on quickly and then let him run off to the school building to meet with his friends who were arriving at the same time.

Cassie laughed at her son's enthusiasm and walked in behind him, saying hi to her coworkers who also taught at the school. Meanwhile, Ben was already seated on the floor in a group of his friends. In front of them sat a woman with a large, leather-bound book in her hands. Ben hardly noticed her, though, because he was in the thick of conversation with his best friend, Ryan.

Ryan and Ben had known each other for several years, which felt like a lifetime for them. Even their parents were friends! That night, since it wasn't a school night, Ben was going to be staying the over at Ryan's house after the event, and he couldn't be more excited! The two of them were in the middle of the group, talking about their plans for the evening, which, so far, included lots of snacks and playing some of their favorite games.

The teacher who had been tasked with organizing the event was up front trying to get everyone's attention so their guest could get started with the stories. It took her a couple tries, but finally the crowd quieted down, and the woman opened her book to begin.

"Are you scared of ghosts?" she asked dramatically.

This won't be scary at all, Ben thought to himself.

The evening wore on, and Ben's confidence secretly wavered. The first story was about a skeleton who walked around complaining about the cold. That was a creepy image, but Ben took comfort knowing there was no way it was real. Then, she told one about a man who disappeared after he claimed his house was haunted. Still creepy, but not too crazy. The one that got to Ben, though, was the one about the ghost in the attic.

This story started a little differently than the others. After telling several from her book, the storyteller closed the it and set it down beside her on the floor.

"For this one," she began, "I'm about to tell you a story that is 100% true. I know it is, because I was there."

The kids didn't know it, but the adults sitting in the back silently snickered at this line and the reaction it got from the audience. A murmur spread through the group on the floor as they speculated whether they were actually going to hear a true story. Ben was skeptical, but he was feeling a *little* concerned for what they were about to be told.

The storyteller began weaving a spooky story about an old house on a hill where she grew up in Arborville. This detail caught Ben's attention because that was where his older cousin, Blake, was living now. Unlike the other stories, this was an actual place he had heard of. He'd even been there!

The story was about a house that many had lived in over the years and, in fact, someone had died in. At this, many of the kids were already wide-eyed (not Ben, of course). She continued, recounting the tale of her childhood home that had been the site of an old man's death many years before. Since his death, she explained, no one had stayed in the house for more than a year.

Then she went on to talk about the many creepy occurrences that she experienced as a kid growing up there. From moving furniture to creaks in the night and even a sighting of a glowing man wandering the halls one stormy night. She told each story with the enthusiasm and passion of someone performing on Broadway, and the whole crowd, parents included, were locked in.

Finally, she concluded with the tale of how she and her sister defeated the ghost by finding his glasses that had been hidden in an old dresser and throwing them out. This, she said, put a stop to the ghost's antics for good.

"We decided he must have been angry that we were keeping his glasses, so we buried them in the backyard. With that, the hauntings stopped."

By this point, Ben was admittedly spooked. It just sounded so *real*. He glanced at Ryan to see if he had any reaction, and his friend looked nervous, too, but he was clearly trying to hide it. The storyteller finished the story and got a round of applause, largely driven by the adult crowd in the back. She took a bow and gave the floor back to a teacher, who thanked everyone for coming and dismissed the audience.

All of Ben's friends immediately started talking amongst themselves, debating the validity of the stories they heard, especially the last one.

"Do you think that was real?"

"It sounded pretty real."

"That had to be made up!"

"I wonder if my house is haunted."

Ben stayed quieter than normal as he rethought some of his beliefs about ghosts. The conversation quickly moved on, though, and he shook off his jitters from the spooky story. He and Ryan went right back to plotting out their evening of fun while they waited for their moms to finish talking to each other. Didn't they know the night was fading fast?

Finally, the adults were done with their conversation, and Ben was free to grab his overnight bag from the truck. It was loaded down with more games than actual traveling essentials, but his mom had made sure he at least brought a change of clothes and a toothbrush. Ben lugged the small duffle bag over to the car Ryan came in and took his spot next to Ryan in the back seat.

"I thought we'd have pizza tonight, if that's alright with you all." Ryan's mom said as she got in the driver's seat, knowing that they would, in fact, be very alright with it. The two friends responded enthusiastically, knowing she'd be getting it from their favorite pizza place, and Ryan's mom laughed a little at their excitement.

"Good. I already had Matthew pick up a couple from Gammereli's, so he should have them when we get home."

Ben's enthusiasm faded slightly. He liked Ryan's older brother fine, but sometimes he was kind of boring. He never wanted to hang out with them. Ben just chalked it up to him being a high schooler, thinking how his two older sisters also got more boring for a while when they were in high school. Now, of course, they both lived far away.

This year was the first one that it was just Ben and his parents at home, and it had felt a little weird for him so far. Usually, his family did all of their Fall traditions together, but with Hannah and Lucy gone, the fun wasn't quite the same. On top of that, they had just moved into a new house, so there were several traditions they didn't even do this year. Their house wasn't even decorated for the Fall season yet, and that was *very* unusual.

That was another fun thing about staying over at Ryan's house: it felt very normal. They had been doing this for years on random weekends throughout the school year. Although, this year was one of the first that Ryan hadn't really come over to Ben's house at all. His parents insisted it was still not ready since the move, so Ryan's parents happily hosted Ben a few more times over the past few months.

Ben was very familiar with the routine of eating pizza and watching a movie or TV show before Ryan's parents went to bed. After that, Ryan and Ben would usually stay up as late as they wanted, as long as they weren't too loud. They hardly ever interacted with Matthew unless he was poking his head in to ask them to quiet down (to Ben's annoyance). He hoped Matthew wouldn't get onto them again tonight.

Ryan didn't live far from the school, so it was a short drive. Seeing Matthew's car in the driveway, they knew the pizza was already there, so they shot out of the car quickly and made a beeline for the dining room. There, two pizza boxes were stacked neatly on the table, and Matthew had apparently already retreated to his own room. Unbothered by his absence, Ryan and Ben tore into the pizza, grabbing a couple slices each of pepperoni and settling on the living room couch almost before Ryan's mom had even walked through the front door.

"Wow, did those stories scare up an appetite for you two?" she asked, laughing. This prompted a chorus of denial from the two friends, who were in the middle of deciding what they would watch that night.

They landed on some old episodes of *Scooby-Doo* that featured the spookiest ghosts, which were perfect for the season. Ryan's mom joined them with her pizza a few minutes into the first episode, saying, "Oh, this one is my favorite!"

They watched through several episodes, laughing at the same parts they always laughed at but still acting surprised when the culprit was unmasked. Ben was having fun, but he did feel like he wasn't enjoying it as much as usual. *It must be that ghost lady. She got me all spooked!* He thought to himself, not wanting to admit it aloud. In the back of his mind, though, he also registered that those episodes were also some of his sisters' favorites that they had watched with him growing up.

After going through several episodes and rounds of pizza, Ryan's dad made it home from work, so they paused the show to greet him. Ryan recounted all of the ghost stories for him, one after the other, and asked him if he thought there was any way they could be true.

Ryan's dad laughed a little, but then got more serious, "Well," he started, "I've told your mom for years now that I think our house may be haunted." Ryan and Ben went wide-eyed and their jaws dropped.

"Really?" Ben asked. Ryan's dad nodded, trying to hide the mischievous look in his eyes.

"Oh yeah! I've seen some wild things up in the attic, especially. That's why we don't ever let you all wander around up there."

At this, his wife nudged him hard from the side and said, "Stop that!" He put his hands up in surrender. "Just be careful is all I'm saying."

With that, the two of them decided to go on to bed (did adults not believe in fun anymore), so they said goodnight to the boys and retreated from the living room.

Now on their own, Ben and Ryan went up to Ryan's room on the second floor to play games and watch some more *Scooby-Doo*. After talking with Ryan's dad, Ben was acutely aware that the attic door was just outside Ryan's door in the ceiling, but he quickly shook the thought away.

He hoped that would be the end of it, but they were hardly into a game of checkers when they heard something above them.

Thump

Thump

Thump

Creeeeaaakkkk

They went quiet for a moment, listening for more.

"What was that?" Ben asked finally. Ryan didn't say anything, still listening.

"Your dad was just messing with us, right?"

No response.

"I mean, even if there was a ghost, it's in the attic, so it wouldn't matter for us anyway, right?"

"Ben, shhhh! I'm trying to listen."

They went silent again, trying to hear any other noises.

Crash!

"Ok, I think we should tell your parents!" Ben said, putting on his bravest face. "What if it's a robber or something?"

"It's not a robber. I don't think." Ryan said, hesitantly.

CRASH!

This time both boys jumped at the loud noise and started talking quickly about what to do. Just then, Ryan's door opened, causing them to jump again.

"What are you all doing?"

It was Matthew, looking to discover the source of the noise.

"Nothing! It's the gho-" Ryan stopped himself before he said it.

Matthew looked at them for a moment before saying, "Ah, Dad's been telling stories, huh?"

As he was speaking, another *thump* came from upstairs. Matthew glanced up and said, "That does not seem to be you two, though."

Without another word, he moved out into the hall and pulled the attic door down by its string, unfolding the attached steps. Ben and Ryan followed him out in the hall as he began to climb.

Noticing his audience, Matthew turned and said, "Well, are you all coming?"

Ben could at least admit to himself that he was frightened at this point. He wasn't sure it was a ghost, necessarily, but whatever was making those loud noises was not something he wanted to cross paths with. On the other hand, there was no way he was going to admit his fright to Ryan's older brother, so he began to climb the steps behind Matthew.

Behind him, Ryan sighed to himself but followed when there was room on the ladder.

They ascended into the dark room above, and the musty smell of old wood and insulation filled their nostrils. It was a large enough space that they could all stand up straight with some room to spare, and there were enough plywood boards for them to walk around on. Moonlight through a dusty window provided just enough light to see the silhouettes of boxes piled up all around.

"Hello?" Matthew called out. There was no response.

He shrugged his shoulders and crossed over to where a light switch was fixed onto a post and flipped it on. Soft light spilled into the attic from the singular light bulb hanging above. They were still for a beat, taking in the room, looking for the cause of the commotion. Slowly the three of them walked around, looking between stacks of boxes. The boards creaked loudly beneath them as they moved.

They moved about quietly, trying to stay alert for whatever they might run into. Matthew didn't appear to be very concerned, but the younger boys were visibly jumpy. They didn't find anything unusual, though, except for one stack of boxes that had been toppled over, and a few books that seemed to have been knocked off the stacks they'd been in.

"Well, that looks like the noises we heard," Matthew said, scanning the room, "but I'm not sure what knocked them over."

Ryan looked around nervously, "This sounds like a ghost to me."

Matthew shook his head, "No, I don't think so..."

Ben frowned and continued looking behind the stacks of boxes. *If it wasn't the ghost, then what-*

Suddenly his thoughts were interrupted by a flash of white flying at his face from behind the nearest box! He screamed and stumbled backwards as the apparent apparition *whooshed* by his head and flew towards Ryan and Matthew. They shouted loudly and dove to the floor, covering their faces. Ben looked back and saw what looked like a flying sheet zooming around the room, bumping into boxes and rafters. The room settled, and the sheet dropped to the ground, moving sporadically on the floor.

"Wait a second," Matthew said, moving towards the sheet. In one quick motion he grabbed it and pulled it upwards to reveal a small bird underneath.

"It's just a bird!" he laughed. There was a pause while reality caught up to Ben and Ryan before they joined in on the laughter, and soon, all three of them were cackling loudly.

"I guess this was your ghost!" Matthew said, nudging Ryan. The bird just watched them nervously, twittering softly as it got used to its newfound freedom.

"It looks scared," Ryan said, "It must have gotten stuck up here somehow."

Ben looked over at the window and saw that it was cracked open, just big enough for a bird to sneak in.

"Look!" he pointed, "Someone left the window open."

"That was me I'm afraid."

The three of them whipped around to see whose voice that was and saw Ryan's dad climbing up through the attic entrance.

"I wanted to see what all the commotion was about," he explained with a laugh, "but it looks like you all have this under control."

While they spoke, the bird nearly made itself dizzy looking back and forth at each person who spoke, trying to assess the situation. It chirped impatiently, as if to draw their attention back. Everyone looked at it for a beat, unsure what to do.

"We should let it out, right?" Ryan asked finally.

Matthew nodded, "Yes, but I'm not sure if it'll just fly out of the window, and I doubt it'll let us near enough to help."

Ryan's dad made a move toward the bird, but it jumped away and scurried in a corner. Before anyone else could try, Ben moved in its direction, picking up the sheet.

"Ben..." Ryan's dad started, but Ben was already getting close. He gently lowered his hands, covered by the sheet. The bird (Ben had named him "Rob" in his head, since "Robin" was the only kind of bird he knew of) jumped slightly but less than before, and as Ben's hands lowered fully to the floor, Rob began cautiously moving to them. He tested the platform with his right foot, and when he decided it was safe, jumped on. Ben slowly and carefully moved his hands and carried Rob to the window and stretched his hands close to the opening.

Rob chirped excitedly and jumped as if to take off. Before he did, though, he turned to Ben and looked at him for a second. Ben held his breath along with everyone else that was watching them. The only sound in the attic was a low whistle from the cool wind outside.

Rob broke the stillness by jerking his head down and pecking at the sheet covering Ben's hands twice. Ben had hardly processed the "thank you" before Rob quickly turned around and leapt out the window into the moonlit night. Ben glanced back at the others and saw that Ryan looked like he was going to pass out, Matthew was stifling a laugh, and Ryan's dad had a proud look that only a dad could pull out at a time like this.

"Good job, Ben," he said. "You're quite the bird - or maybe, ghost - whisperer."

The comment elicited a good laugh out of the three boys, even Matthew. Satisfied with the joke's reception, Ryan's dad invited them all back downstairs to enjoy some hot chocolate and climbed back down the ladder.

They all walked back across the creaky boards and one by one lowered themselves down the ladder into the hallway below. Matthew went down first and helped the other two as they hopped off.

"Good job with the bird," he said to Ben while he folded the ladder back up. "You're a pretty cool kid."

"Thanks for taking us up there to track it down. You're a pretty cool *kid*, too," Ben replied with a smirk. That got a laugh from Matthew, and he gave Ben a fist bump to show his respect for the dig. The two of them followed Ryan down the stairs, trying to be quiet since it was late. In the kitchen, Ryan's dad was finishing up the hot chocolates and started passing them around.

Matthew turned back to Ben, "How are your sisters doing? I know Hannah's in college now, and Lucy moved for a job, right?"

Ben frowned at the question. He had forgotten that Matthew was nearly Hannah's age and that they were friends.

"They're fine, I think," he replied. "I haven't really talked to them a whole lot since they moved."

"Ah, I understand," Matthew said, nodding. "Well, when you get a chance, you should definitely tell them about this. I'm sure they'd love to hear about your ghost-hunting adventures."

"Oh, is that what you all were doing up there?" Ryan's dad said, passing a mug of hot chocolate to Matthew. "Well, if that wasn't the ghost, I guess it's still out there!" Saying this he jumped at Ryan, who just laughed (prompting Matthew to make a "shhhh" sound like a tire losing air).

The four of them continued to talk while they sipped their hot chocolates. Ben loved the warmth it poured into him and the way the marshmallows tasted after they'd soaked up the chocolate drink. When the mugs were empty, Ryan's dad carefully placed them in the dishwasher and said goodnight again, this time making the boys promise to go on to bed.

The three of them went back upstairs and did go to bed - after a round or two of checkers and Mariokart. Matthew even joined in on the fun, and Ben could tell Ryan was happy for the extra company. Before he fell asleep that night, Ben decided he would give his sisters a call when he got home the next day.

After the long night, Ben and Ryan both slept in longer than usual, and when they finally stirred, Ben saw that it was almost time for his mom to pick him up. By the time she arrived at the house, Ben and Ryan were snacking on cold pizza for breakfast (a sleepover classic), and Ben was already packed up to leave. Ryan's mom was sipping on coffee and listening to the now very dramatic stories from the night before

"It sounds like you all had an exciting night," Ben's mom laughed as they quickly recounted the highlights for her.

"I know, I can't believe I slept through it!" said Ryan's mom.

Ben finished the slice he was working on and got his bag as his mom thanked Ryan's again for letting Ben stay, promising Ryan could come over as soon as the new house was ready. With that, Ben and his mom stepped out into the cool, autumn air, waving behind them to Ryan and his mom.

Ben heard his mom saying something about Dad fixing something at home, but he was distracted by movement from the tree in the front yard. A bird zipped from a lower branch and onto the truck as they were approaching it to get in.

"It's Rob!" Ben cried. He'd recognize that bird anywhere.

"Rob, huh?" his mom mumbled, surprised at the newcomer. She cleared her throat and stuck out her hand towards the bird as if to shake its hand.

"How do you do, Rob? I'm Cassie, Ben's mother."

"Mom!" Ben yelled, laughing at her. Rob tilted his head and chirped, confused at the gesture. Then he focused on Ben, hopped once, chirped loudly, and flew off again.

"Bye!" Ben called out, waving to the bird.

On the way home, Ben was already crafting the way he'd tell the story to his sisters. Cassie could see the gears turning in his head as he looked out the window at the fall scenery they were driving past. She smiled to herself, thankful for the pure joy of childhood adventures.

What goes bump in the night?

What creaks and groans

And haunts the dark

Corners of our lives?

We hear phantoms

And ghosts

And malicious ghouls

But, mostly

When you

Look close

You find

A *friend*

- *C.E.*

Autumn Storm

As he raked, Bill was thankful for the cooler weather. It seemed like it had taken forever to come, but now it was there in full swing with a cool breeze lazily pulling at the last few leaves clinging to mostly-bare tree limbs. He had already raked as many leaves as he could earlier in the season, but late October brought a new wave of red, orange, and brown that had tumbled onto the lawn below.

It had been a stormy couple of weeks, and when the last system blew through a few days before, it had thrown a lot of the leaves to the ground that had stubbornly been hanging on to the tree limbs above. Now, the lawn was once again covered, and it was driving Bill crazy seeing them there. That morning, he had gotten up to sit on the porch swing and enjoy the cool breeze, but seeing those leaves scattered about finally got to him. Soon he was out in the yard raking them into small piles.

That morning was cool but not unbearably so with a light coat. The breeze was just strong enough to be felt, but gentle enough to be refreshing. Bill enjoyed the soft light that distilled through the gray clouds overhead, and he was glad to be outdoors. The pain in his knees made it take longer than usual to fetch the rake from the shed, but he slowly made his way back to the front lawn to start his chore.

Bill rhythmically passed the old garden rake over the ground and let the leaves heap up over and over. He enjoyed the work, as always, but his arms and knees still ached. Bill hid his grimace and gritted his teeth. He'd hoped it wouldn't hurt as much as it did, but apparently the fall he'd had the week before had been harder than he thought. Although, it seems to have been about as hard as his son, James, insisted it had been. Bill hoped he could rake the leaves up before James made it over there to take over the job. Just as he was getting into a rhythm of pushing through the pain, however, he heard a voice behind him call out, "Save some for the rest of us!"

He turned to see his son and daughter-in-law climbing out of their truck and walking towards him. *Uh-oh*, he thought to himself. They'd gotten there quicker than he had expected.

"Didn't we say we'd take care of it?" James asked, reaching out for the rake.

"Well, you know me. It was driving me crazy seeing them all piled up out here," Bill replied, "Besides, it's a nice day to be out."

"A nice day to sit on the porch," Brooke chimed in next to him. "Go on, sit on the swing for a minute and let us handle it. Besides, it's the least we can do after you raked our yard with Bailey."

They continued back and forth like this for a couple minutes, but ultimately, the aches joined the young people's side and convinced Bill that it was time for a break.

Despite the protests in his head, Bill handed off the rake and slowly climbed up the stairs to the porch swing, secretly glad for some rest. He sank onto the old, wooden swing that overlooked the yard and let the two of them handle the leaves. He wanted to grumble and complain about having his work taken from him, but sitting down did bring relief to his joints. Maybe he'd stay on the swing for just a few minutes before trying to jump back in.

As he gently swung on the porch swing, the breeze gently waved the windchimes hanging next to him and made them sing a soft song that washed over the mid-autumn day. Occasionally, the sun would peek through the blanket of gray overhead and split the afternoon chill with warmth and golden light. The rhythm of the rakes gathering the leaves together tied the scene together nicely.

Bill was no longer jumping headlong into leaf piles like he used to, but he greatly enjoyed watching his son and daughter-in-law playfully pushing each other into the piles as they worked. It was very peaceful. The only thing that was missing were his grandchildren, but James had told him ahead of time that their two youngest were out with friends today.

The other two had moved away, of course, and Bill often wished they'd come back to visit more, especially on a day like today. He felt memories of past Autumns wash over him stronger than they had in months, and they made him miss his older grandsons even more. Usually raking the leaves at their house was a good excuse to pay a visit when everyone had still lived there.

Bill felt a pang thinking about the month before when he had raked their lawn, remembering his youngest granddaughter cannonballing into the piles he'd built. Now, he felt sad, thinking about the difficulty he had just raking a few leaves in his own yard. He continued to watch James and Brooke gather the rust-colored leaves in piles on the edge of the yard, wishing he was out there with them.

As he sat watching, the gray sky above overtook the few rays of sun and began to darken. The windchimes blew around a little more frantically as the clouds sent a chilly blast of wind down. Bill looked intently at the sky and thought he felt a couple small drops blow onto the porch.

James and Brooke had nearly finished raking the leaves into the burn pile on the edge of the yard when a few large drops found their way to the ground. Bill felt a few more drops blow onto the porch, so he abandoned his post on the swing and retreated to the warmth inside, calling behind him for the other two to follow him in. They joined him a few moments later. Only a handful of drops had hit them, but they made a big show of being thankful for the coffee and tea Bill had already started to make to warm them up.

Bill's wife, Martha, was in the kitchen making lunch already and asked James and Brooke if they'd like to join. They confirmed that they didn't have too much going on that day with the kids not being home, so they agreed to stay for lunch and a round or two of cards. The smell of lunch cooking filled the room, making the warmth inside contrast sharply with the dismal scene outside.

The four of them gathered around the table in the sunroom as the sound of cards shuffling and rain pattering on the windows trickled through the room. They all drank their warm beverage of choice and felt the level of coziness in the room rise with the temperature. The lazy shower outside drummed persistently on the tin roof above, just loud enough to hear. The afternoon ticked away and the four of them settled into their game with no sense of urgency as they ate lunch and played.

Suddenly, as James was playing his hand, the lights flickered several times. They all looked out the window at once and saw that the storm had gotten more intense in the time they'd been sitting there. The wind was blowing hard, ripping the last of the leaves off some of the trees out in the yard and bending branches this way and that. Now that they had stopped talking, they could hear the wind chime being violently rattled around.

They all shared a look, and James started to play again when the power cut out entirely.

"Well, I wasn't expecting that," he said, putting his cards down.

Bill's eyes were adjusting to the sudden darkness, clinging to the little bit of light that came through the windows from outside.

"Will the kids be ok?" he asked, now gazing out the window more intently.

"They should be. Bailey and Leo are at friends' houses, and I don't think the storm is supposed to go towards Sam or Oliver." James said, checking the radar on his phone.

Brooke was already on her phone, texting the two kids who were in town. A minute later she confirmed that they hadn't even lost power where they were, and she made each of them promise to take shelter if it got much worse, and to avoid the windows. James assured her that it wouldn't get that bad, and he asked Bill if they had any flashlights to brighten the place up a bit in the meantime.

Bill thought for a moment and said he thought there would be some flashlights and lanterns in the basement. The two of them walked carefully down the creaky steps into the unfinished basement, using James' phone as a dim light to see the steps. In the dark basement, they could still hear thunder rumbling overhead.

"Goodness," James said, "This came out of nowhere."

Bill decided not to point out that the weather channel had called for rain ahead of time - though, to be fair, it wasn't supposed to be quite this bad or come so early in the day.

The two of them searched through several tool boxes and drawers for the flashlights Bill had mentioned, but they weren't having any luck. Sifting through his collection of old tools and keepsakes that were kept in the basement, Bill was a little self-conscious of the mess. He'd been meaning to get rid of a lot of those old things. If James thought anything about it, he didn't let on, though.

After several minutes of searching, they found one electric lantern, two large flashlights, one small flashlight, and a few kerosene lamps.

"Wow, these are practically antiques!" James said, holding one up.

Bill frowned a little at the comment, thinking how it felt like yesterday they had bought those lamps, but he caught enough admiration in James' tone to not take it too personally.

"Old reliable," he said. "Those lamps have been used through many blackouts here. Do you remember using those when you were younger?"

James tilted his head and thought for a second, "Yeah, yeah I think I do. Well, I remember being told not to roughhouse around them, anyway."

Bill chuckled at the memory of snatching one of the lamps away from a pair of wrestling, young boys, afraid the log house would go up in flames if they weren't careful.

"I think we should use them!" James said suddenly, and he started searching for some kerosene to fill it with.

Just then they heard Brooke's voice call down the stairs.

"Have you all found us some light or are we going to be sitting in the dark all afternoon?"

"We have the lights. I'm just getting some kerosene for the lamps!" James called back.

"Kerosene?"

At that Brooke stepped slowly down the stairs, carefully using the rail to keep herself from falling down them. James held up one of the flashlights and shined it on the lamps they had found, and Brooke got excited about them. Bill hadn't really considered the "vibe" the lamps would create, but apparently it would be a cool one.

They soon found the kerosene cans, and next to them was something big and bulky underneath a canvas tarp. Letting curiosity get the best of him, James threw off the cloth to reveal an old, dusty piano underneath.

"Is this yours?" Brooke asked Bill, inquisitively.

"It's Martha's, actually. She used to be quite the player! We haven't gotten that out in years, though."

"I'd almost forgotten about that!" They heard from the stairs as Martha came down behind them. Not wanting to be left out, she had followed after Brooke when she went down.

"Can you still play?" James asked his mom.

Martha hesitated for a moment before going over to the keys and tapping a few.

"Maybe."

Almost automatically, she pulled out and dusted off the old bench that was tucked up underneath the piano and sat down. She paused for just a moment before tapping out a short, light tune. The light from the flashlights didn't quite light up the room on their own, but she hardly had to look at the keys while she played. The others were entranced by the melody, and Bill felt his heart leap seeing his wife of 50 years create music like she had when they first got married.

When she finished, the others clapped furiously and cheered, "Encore! Encore!" She happily obliged, feeling the rush that came with playing. As she continued onto another song,

James started setting up the kerosene lanterns, bathing the room in a warm glow.

The music almost seemed to fuel the tiny flames, causing them to burn brighter and happier. By the time she finished her second piece, the others had found a couple old chairs and an old loveseat that had been stored down there to sit on while they listened. Without a word, Martha played right into the next song, hardly missing a note as she went.

Bill felt the music dance around them, growing into a bright bloom from the piano and spilling warm light over everything. It wove in and around the small audience, and the chilly air melted into warmth as the music painted vibrant colors in their minds.

Deep bass notes swelled into navy clouds, while the higher notes dripped through the air like splashes of bright blue paint. Somewhere in the middle, Martha found swirls of gold that spun playfully from the ivory keys and joined the glow of the kerosene lamps.

Bill took it all in and sighed contently to himself. Somehow, he felt like the music itself soothed his achy joints that had been sore from descending the stairs a few minutes before. More than that, the discontentment that had been plaguing his mind for the past couple weeks seemed to be fading, as well, even if just for a moment. The relief was almost overwhelming.

By the fourth song, Bill had tears welling up in his eyes that he tried furiously to fight back. James noticed but didn't say anything and just rested his hand on his dad's shoulder. James knew that the last year had been difficult with his sister moving further away and several of the grandkids growing up and going to college or moving away themselves. That was not even to mention the last week or so that Bill had spent struggling with his own body.

Bill was always so supportive of everyone as they grew up and settled into life, but he often missed them and missed being in their lives more. In that moment, though, he felt an incredible and unexpected peace as Martha's music bounced off the basement walls and gently hugged the group together. He was proud of his family, and he was so happy to be with them.

When Martha finished her fifth piece, the others gave her a standing ovation this time, at which she did a small bow. She said she needed a break from playing, and Brooke decided to step in since she'd been trying to learn piano and hadn't gotten a chance to practice in a while.

For the next hour, they stayed gathered in the lamplight as Brooke and Martha traded off turns playing the old piano. James and Bill even jumped in a couple times to tap out a simple tune or two they'd learned years ago. Bill felt the music continue to wash over his achy joints and loosen them as he sat with his family in the dimly-lit basement. It was impossibly cozy for such a stormy afternoon.

James was stretching out his fingers dramatically, as if he was about to play an incredible sonnet, when the lights flickered on once, then twice, and stayed on the third time. The room was now flooded with a harsher, white light that caused everyone to blink hard as their eyes adjusted.

"I guess my concert's over," James laughed, getting to his feet and taking a deep bow. Bill laughed along with the others but silently wished for more time by the lamplight. They all put out the lanterns, though, and climbed back upstairs. Bill felt like the steps might have been a little easier to take than they were earlier.

Through the windows, they could see that the outside world was soaked but calm. It was as if the storm had taken all the wind with it, leaving a few wispy clouds hanging in the sky that just barely covered the sun. Bill was almost disappointed to see that the storm had moved out, but as his son and daughter-in-law got ready to leave, he found himself filled with the warmth of the past few hours. He smiled and waved as they hugged him and Martha and walked out the door. They waved to James and Brooke while they climbed into their car and told them to come back anytime.

Later, Bill heard piano music drift up the stairs from the basement and realized it was Martha, tapping out one of the

melodies from earlier, and he went to watch her play. He smiled to himself thinking of his family gathered around the old piano, singing and laughing during the mini-concert. Maybe it was time to have someone move that piano upstairs again and get it properly re-tuned. The thought of Martha's music filling the room at Thanksgiving in a few weeks made him smile even wider.

Things had changed a lot for him in the past couple of years, but he was thankful for the wonderful memories that he could still create with his family. He was looking forward to many more to come.

With ivory keys she
Sowed the field
By oil lamps her
Work was known

With steadfast love
She fed the crop
With boundless joy
They worked together

From warmth and light
The earth yielded
Beautiful, sweet fruit
And a melodious garden

Gentle people are healed by the plentiful harvest

- C.E.

Tricks or Treats by Any Other Name

Charlie was more nervous than usual this Halloween. That day at work, he ran through the plan in his mind for that evening, checking and double checking it for flaws or problems. Normally he didn't consider himself to be an overthinker, but this year was different.

This year his family was in a new neighborhood, and, although he considered himself to be a people person, he hadn't really met anyone they lived near. Between long nights at work recently and long weekends settling the house, his time had felt fully booked since they moved. Not that meeting new people was the easiest thing with a clear schedule, but a full one didn't make it any easier.

This isn't a problem for a lot of people. Plenty of Charlie's friends and co-workers don't know their neighbors and like it that way. For Charlie, though, he felt more at home (and more comfortable) when he knew who he was around. That was something that was important to him, especially when he was sending his son off to trick or treat at their houses.

It hadn't helped that they had run into problems since day one in their new home. From leaky pipes to broken water heaters, Charlie had felt like he'd spent days just on the repairs they needed, not to mention the unpacking and general adjusting to the new area. They'd just moved across the city, but they were no longer near many of their favorite restaurants or parks, so they were constantly having to find new places to frequent.

For Charlie, all of this culminated on that night of the year when they were going to be sending their youngest out to the houses around them for trick or treating. That's not to mention their niece and Ben's friend, Ryan, who were coming over since they didn't live in a neighborhood good for walking around in.

Trick or treating wasn't new for them, of course. When their daughters, Hannah and Lucy, were younger, they spent every Halloween doing trunk-or-treat at church and joining friends to trick-or-treat in their neighborhoods. The girls had long outgrown the tradition and no longer lived with them, but their son, Ben, was still young enough for another year or two of soliciting candy from their neighbors.

This year, though, they were somewhere unfamiliar, and being responsible for not only their son but also Ryan and Bailey going to strangers' houses had Charlie feeling a little anxious about it all. His wife, Cassie, insisted that this would be a good way to meet neighbors and that it would be fun for the kids. Charlie had a hard time refuting the logic. Still, in small breaks at work that day, Charlie couldn't help but re-scan through all the crime and safety reports for the area. After the 7th time looking through it all, he felt decently satisfied, but he was still nervous.

That evening after work, he and Cassie had gotten their youngest one all dressed up and armed with a basket to collect candy before going out into the subdivision. She whispered quiet affirmations for Charlie about how great the evening would go, seeing that he was nervous, but it didn't quite comfort him completely. Charlie was not used to living so close to so many people like this. He grew up off a narrow highway where the nearest house was a quarter mile away on each side.

Up until that point, their family had lived in a similar place, but now they were in a subdivision where if you threw a baseball wrong, you'd knock out your neighbor's window. That made him feel, well, watched, maybe? At the very least, he felt more protective of the three kids in their care tonight as they got ready, and he made sure to layer Ben in an extra shirt or two so he wouldn't get too cold.

His wife, Cassie, had offered to take Ben, Ryan, and Bailey around to all the houses with Bailey's mom, Brooke, if he would stay back and hand out candy to the kids that came by their house. Instinctively, Charlie wanted to go and be with the kids when they went to the houses, but he knew Cassie specifically wanted to meet the neighbors on their walk. He also knew that she was less likely to crowd the kids like he would, so he resigned to meet neighbors as they visited their house.

Again, not being used to having that many neighbors, he had never really handed out candy like this before, but he made sure to stock the best sweets, and a lot of them, for whoever came by that evening. He also decided to build a fire in the small fire pit they had towards the end of the driveway where he could hand out candy and watch for his own family's return.

Bailey and her mom, Brooke, arrived right as it was getting dark outside, ready to join the circuit of kids and parents circling the block in search of candy. Brooke told Charlie that her husband, James, Cassie's brother, would come by, too, after he got off work that evening, but they didn't have long to chat before the kids dragged them out the door and down the street.

The trio of kids was a sight to see as they left. Ben was dressed as a fearsome pirate, coordinating with Ryan who was dressed as a rival pirate captain, and Bailey was Velma from Scooby-Doo. Cassie and Brooke laughed as Velma tried to convince the pirates to look for clues, and Charlie chuckled to himself at the scene.

He watched them for just a moment longer before going out to arrange the logs and kindling together in the firepit he'd set up. He lit the tinder and carefully poked and blew on the sparks until a fire sprang up among the kindling. He hoped it would grow quickly, as the Autumn chill had already set in since the sun set. Fortunately, the fire did catch quick, and Charlie sank into his old lawn chair to let it warm him up. He had barely been sitting in the chair for thirty seconds when he heard children coming towards him from down the street.

"Trick or treat!" He heard as they got closer.

He smiled and dropped handfuls of candy into each bag and bucket that was presented to him. He looked down at the load of candy he was holding and wondered if he had bought quite enough for the evening.

"That's a good fire you have going there," he heard behind him, as he was thinking.

Turning, Charlie saw his neighbor from the house next door walking up his own driveway towards him. Unfortunately, whoever built these houses put the driveways directly next to each other. Charlie did not like the set up, and the proximity of the stranger coming towards him nearly startled him. He was used to it being more of an event for a neighbor to wander over, rather than it being as easy as walking down the driveway.

Apprehensive though he felt, he did recognize the chance to finally meet someone they lived nearby.

"Thank you," he responded to the man, "I've done a lot of camping, so I have experience."

The older man chuckled and said, "I used to do a lot of camping, myself. Mind if I join you?"

"Not at all. Pull up a chair."

Charlie folded out one of the other lawn chairs he'd brought for his family for the man to sit in. He thanked Charlie and sat down.

"Name's Byron," he said, reaching out his hand to shake Charlie's.

"Mine's Charlie, good to meet you."

Byron also had a bucket of candy and asked if he could hand it out there with him, to which Charlie agreed. The two started talking, just small talk at first, but soon they were getting to know each other a little more.

"So, do you have any kids or grandkids trick or treating here tonight?" Charlie asked.

"No, no," Byron laughed, "My kids live a few towns over, so they're walking around some neighborhoods over there."

"Are they going to stop by tonight sometime?"

"No, we never really did much for Halloween. I just enjoy handing out candy around here."

As they talked, the moon peeked out from behind the clouds and showered light on the neighborhood and the small, costumed figures that wandered from house to house. Byron noticed Charlie scanning the streets and asked if he was nervous.

"A little," he admitted, "It's our first year in this neighborhood, and my wife is out with the kids. I just want to know they're safe."

Byron assured him that the neighborhood had always been very safe, and his kids had always had a good time there when they were growing up. Charlie found out that they had lived there for many years. Apparently Byron really loved that area.

"It's just very pretty here," Byron said. "I love being outside, sitting on the porch, walking around the neighborhood, or even just doing yard work and mowing."

"Yeah, I have really enjoyed that too." Charlie replied. "I've noticed your garden. It's really impressive, from the outside at least."

Byron thanked him and said, "It's my pride and joy."

Charlie had seen the garden when they moved in and was always intrigued by it. It was a small piece of the backyard that was full of plants and trees from what Charlie could see, but it was fully surrounded on all sides by a tall, brick wall. A few flowers and vines poked up above the wall, but most of the garden was hidden within. There also didn't seem to be a door or gate anywhere, which intrigued Charlie even more. When he was younger, his curiosity might have provoked him to climb the wall just to see what was inside. As it was, though, he still didn't have a clue what those walls guarded.

He almost let the conversation die there, but finally he asked, "What all do you have in there?"

Byron started to answer, but he stopped and instead asked, "Do you want to see?"

Charlie's curiosity couldn't pass up an opportunity to satisfy itself, so of course, he said yes.

Without another word, Byron popped up out of his chair and walked towards the garden, gesturing for Charlie to follow. With no kids around at the moment, Charlie was free to join him, so he followed, leaving the candy out in the open for anyone who might wander through in the meantime.

As they got closer to the garden wall, Charlie saw the thin vines that spread out in web-like patterns across the brick. The moonlight revealed small, colorful blossoms that popped up along the vines, too. In contrast, the brick was a dull, rusty red that seemed to come from a different time and place compared to the modern gray bricks many of the houses in the neighborhood were built with. Now that he thought about it, Charlie realized the bricks of Byron's own house were similarly different than those of the other houses around.

He saw Byron walk around to the right side of the garden and Charlie caught up just in time to see him slip through the wall. Confused, Charlie moved in closer, and in the silver moonlight, he could just see a sliver of wall that separated out from the rest. He tried it, and the section of brick swung inward. Charlie chuckled to himself at the eccentricity of the older man. Hidden doors and secret gardens, what's next!

As he followed the older man through the wall, he was taken aback by how big the garden seemed compared to how it looked from the outside. There were rows of raised beds full of vegetables and separated by a smooth, clear walkway, on which the two walked towards the center. Charlie looked around, seeing how the moon made the bright flowers on the edge seem like they were glowing.

Small, warm lights lit up the pathway near their feet and made everything seem a little more magical. Vines of some sort wound in and among the little lights but didn't venture onto the path, almost as if they were staying out of the way of the old man when he passed. Charlie was especially captivated by a colorful plant that was near the door that he'd never seen before. He couldn't believe all of this was hidden there in plain sight.

Snapping back to the present, Charlie realized he had lost track of Byron while he had been taking everything in. He looked around, craning his neck to see around the plants, but there was no sign of him. Behind him, Charlie heard the secret door thud as it shut, causing Charlie to jump! *Relax*, he thought to himself, *He's just an old man with a green thumb. Just because it's Halloween doesn't mean something spooky is going on.*

Still, he double checked the door to see if it was locked. It swung open with relative ease, so, relaxing again, Charlie ventured back into the garden to catch up with Byron. He searched through the rows of vegetables and flowers, but Byron seemed to have disappeared. As he went, Charlie himself started to feel lost. He spun in a circle, surrounded by greenery. He honestly wasn't quite sure which way was which.

He ran through a quick plan to follow the walls and find his way out if he needed to, but that didn't help him find Byron. His search became a little more frantic as he rushed by flower beds full of irises and tulips (were they even in season?). Finally, he rounded a corner past a wall of tomato vines (those definitely weren't in season now), and there Byron was, sitting on a bench across from a small tree, right in the middle of it all.

Panting a little from his search, Charlie walked over and joined him on the bench.

"You can really move, huh?"

"Oh, I was just excited to get here," Byron laughed. "This is my quiet place."

The two of them sat in silence for a moment, and Charlie could *feel* the quiet Byron was mentioned. Inside those four walls, the noise of the outside world seemed muted, almost nonexistent. Charlie felt a breath fill his lungs and gently flow back out. This felt like the peace he had missed since they moved further into the city. Underneath the small tree in front of them, Charlie saw a rosebush that was quite large. Blooming in the moonlight were buds of all different colors and sizes. Reds, yellows, pinks, and whites glowed and shook in the breeze. They waved like they were welcoming him to their home.

"This is the heart of my garden," Byron said with a misty look in his eyes. Charlie saw emotion fill the man's face and stayed respectfully quiet as he continued.

"Back when we first bought this house, the area all around it was still farmland, and that included this section of the backyard that we had just bought. We seeded most of it with grass and a few trees, but here, the farmer who owned the land before asked us to leave this rosebush. He told us it had grown up naturally, right in the middle of the field. In fact, he told us that he hadn't even tried to be particularly careful around it, but the roses, apparently, are stubborn about their space. He asked us to care for it, and eventually my wife and I built this garden around it. Now, it's a place of quiet rest for me, away from the noise."

Charlie wasn't sure what to say. He must have had an incredulous look on his face because Byron chuckled when he looked back and assured him the story was true. With a small sigh, the older man continued.

"My wife, Linda, was a ray of sunshine. I always told her the plants here could grow by her light alone." He smiled, "She was wonderful and kind, and she loved sharing this garden. It was one of the ways she shared joy."

His smile faded slightly. "She passed a few years ago. Since then, I've had a hard time inviting people in to share. I forgot how much I enjoyed it, too."

Again, Charlie was at a loss for words, but seeing Byron smile at him again, he returned the expression.

"Charlie, you're a good presence. Thank you for sharing some peace with me tonight."

The two of them sat still for what Charlie thought could've been hours but was probably just a few minutes. The breeze was the only thing moving, and with it swayed the small tree and the rosebuds, still glowing in the moonlight. The garden around them moved in a slow rhythm that was mesmerizing to watch. The roses in particular danced like they were putting on a show for the visitors. Charlie could hardly take his eyes away.

After several moments of silence, Byron leaned over and said, almost whispering, "You, my friend, are welcome to visit this place anytime. In fact, you should take a rose or two back for your wife." Charlie was about to object, not wanting to impose, but Byron cut him off, "No, no, I insist. This garden is supposed to be shared, and it's not doing much good if I'm the only one enjoying it. You have been very kind to me this evening. Please, let me return the favor."

Charlie shut his mouth and nodded. "Thank you" seemed like small words for the gesture, but Charlie said them anyway.

Another moment or two passed before Charlie finally asked, "How do you think the roses grew here like that?"

Byron smiled for a second and simply replied, "This is a good place to grow."

Charlie paused for a beat before returning the smile. "Yeah, I think you may be right."

The way out of the garden was much less confusing with Byron leading the way. As they walked down the path back to the door, Charlie thought everything looked even more magical, somehow. He took in the sweet scent of the roses Byron picked out for him and thought about how excited he was to share this with Cassie. They could both use the simple beauty right now.

With the hidden door swinging shut behind them, Charlie caught one last glance at the hidden garden and already wanted to go back in. He heard the next wave of children down the street, though, so the two of them returned to the now-fading fire and got the candy ready.

As they sat back down, Charlie added a log to the flames and asked one last question that was on his mind.

"So, why did you build that big wall around the garden? And how come the door is so secretive?"

Byron laughed at the question and replied, "Well, the wall is a way to make sure it really is a place that is separate from everything else, a true retreat from the world, so to speak. That's not to mention protecting it from hungry animals. As for the door..." At this he chuckled, "That's just an old folk's attempt at a little fun. It always draws a reaction from visitors."

At that, Charlie couldn't help but laugh, having now fully replaced intrigue with admiration for the garden oasis.

Since Byron had sat down, Charlie felt more at peace than before. For the rest of the evening, the two of them talked like old friends by the warm glow of the fire, taking turns prodding the logs to keep it going, and each one giving a handful of candy to whichever superhero or ghost came asking for it. The two continued to talk and laugh until Charlie's family came walking down the street to return.

Byron greeted the kids enthusiastically, dropping some candy in each kid's bag. He introduced himself to everyone quickly but excused himself back to his house, eyeing how late it had gotten. He gave up his chair to one of the kids and walked back inside.

"Who was that?" Cassie, asked.

Charlie simply replied, "A new friend. I've had quite the night." He promised to tell them all about it later, but first, he wanted to hear about their night. The kids enthusiastically told Charlie about all the compliments they got on their costumes and the more interesting ones they saw out and about. Cassie and Brooke confirmed that the neighbors were all very nice, and that they all had a great time. The report confirmed Charlie's feelings of contentment about the evening, and he was happy they had such a good time.

Soon after, Bailey's dad, James, arrived, having just gotten off work, and joined them around the fire. For another hour or so, the six of them roasted marshmallows and sorted through the prizes that weighed down Ben, Ryan, and Bailey's trick or treating baskets. Charlie told them all about the wonderful little garden that was tucked behind the brick walls in Byron's yard, enjoying the wide-eyed reactions from the kids at the more fantastical details he shared. Soon, though, Ryan's mom came to pick him up, and Bailey and her family headed home, too.

That night as they put away the fire pit and wound down for bed, Charlie felt lighter. Cozying back into the warmth of their house, he felt more at home than he had even earlier that evening. There were still plenty of neighbors to meet, but it was a start, and a good start, at that. He had really enjoyed talking with Byron, and now he had a great place to get roses for his Cassie.

The rest of the evening was peaceful as Cassie and Charlie put Ben to bed and relaxed for a minute before heading to bed themselves. As Charlie looked around their house before going to sleep, he thought about everything that needed to be done from general maintenance to big fixes he had yet to even really look at. They hadn't even unpacked all of their boxes yet, leaving their usual fall decor trapped in cardboard somewhere. For at least that night, though, Charlie's attitude towards a lot of the chores was different, and he was excited to continue building their home.

As he finally laid down to rest, Charlie had one last thought before he drifted to sleep:

This really is a good place to grow.

An oasis awaits
In the suburban jungle
Away from repetition
And paved lines

There you find life
And barely-tamed growth
And a gentle breeze
Missing from the world outside

The trees dance with joy
The water speaks peace
The vines inspire contentment
And the roses cheerfully beckon you in

- C.E.

Trees and Bonfires

The reality of my situation set in as the sun set. I was who knows how high above the trees in the middle of the forest, and soon, I would be in total darkness. I willed my body to hop off the tree limb I was sitting on and scramble down the way I came. Fun fact about climbing trees: going down fast can actually be much harder and much more dangerous than going up.

I quickly, but carefully, lowered myself from one branch to the other, being overly cautious about branches that might break underneath me. The light was fading quicker than I thought possible now, and I felt a sense of urgency make my heart race in my chest. I could just make out the forest floor below me, and I relaxed a little, knowing I was close to solid ground. Just then, my foot hit a loose piece of bark that slipped out from under me, and I tumbled down hard. I bounced off a branch or two like one of those Plinko boards at the fair, and instead of landing in a prize slot, I collapsed in a heap at the foot of the tree. For a second, I felt fine and thought I was incredibly lucky, but then it all hit at once.

It seemed to be mostly bruises - bad bruises - and several scrapes where I wasn't covered. My hands may have gotten the brunt of that injury, and they stung with red-hot pain from being scraped by the rough bark. I wished I was back at the creek with its cool water to dunk them in. Pushing myself up, I knew I didn't have time to lay there. It was almost completely dark now, and I had to keep pushing forward.

It steadily got darker as I walked, and soon, I could just see the silhouettes of the trees as I passed them. I had forgotten my coat when I started on my expedition, so I just got colder with the sun gone. I began walking quicker, feeling jumpier than usual as the shadows around me seemed to morph into all sorts of beasts and scary creatures in my mind. The smallest rustle in the leaves made me jump and pick up the pace even more. A couple times my foot snagged on a root or a fallen branch and nearly knocked me over, forcing me to slow down more than I'd liked.

I could barely see three feet in front of me at this point, and if I hadn't been more careful, I would've fallen right off the side of the cliff edge I stumbled out onto! I had noticed the difference in the ground when it switched from dirt to hard rock, and I managed to stop right before I hit the edge. I got down on my hands and knees to figure out where exactly the edge was, and it seemed to stretch out far in both directions. Hopelessly, I sat down and let my feet dangle off the side for a second. *Where do I go now?* Just then, the thick layer of clouds overhead parted and let a sliver of moonlight through, exposing the sight before me.

Stretching out ahead was a small valley that had a river running through it, far below me. The river was sparkling in the brief moonlight, and the trees all around it cast deep shadows. I could see that the cliff I was on did in fact stretch out far in either direction. I also saw that directly below me was a natural staircase of rock jutting out from the cliff that I could easily climb down without injury.

I got to take in the view for another second before the clouds enveloped the moon once again. I sat for another beat, looking out to where the valley had disappeared from view. For a second I thought I saw fireflies blinking in the dark, but it must have been the moonlight lingering in my vision because as the breeze swept cool air over me again, what light I thought I'd seen vanished.

Having now caught my breath, I willed myself to move forward again and cautiously lowered myself down to the next boulder. With that, I was able to slowly crawl down the cliffside from one boulder to the next. The cool rock made me shiver as I climbed. Finally, I reached solid ground at the bottom and practically cheered! I knew I needed to keep moving, though, so I continued on through the forest - now trying to roughly follow the river I saw from above as I remembered it.

Occasionally I would hear the sound of rushing water to my left, giving me an idea of where I was. I tried to avoid going too close to the water so I wouldn't fall in, but a few times I lost track of how close I got nearer to the calm parts of the river, and I accidentally stepped into the edge of the water. I was cold enough as it was, but cold water now flooded my boots and soaked my socks. I just sighed and course-corrected to avoid the water once more. The dark had become suffocating, and at that point, I was trying to dodge trees and push through the undergrowth blindly, desperate to get out of there. I hoped I was getting closer to where I needed to go, closer to...

I stopped suddenly as this thought crossed my mind: *Where was I going?*

I knew I'd been going towards... something. Come to think of it, though, I wasn't really sure what. I turned around, thinking, listening, and trying hard to see anything in the dense darkness. I had to face it. I was completely and utterly lost, and I didn't even know where I was trying to go originally. I sat down in dismay, unsure what direction I should even go in. Was following the river even the right call?

As I sat there, I heard all sorts of noises creep into the woods around me. The sound of rustling leaves and snapping twigs surrounded me, and my heart now threatened to pop out of my chest! Everything sounded like a dangerous animal or a menacing hunter roaming the woods. I became hyper-aware of everything from the direction of the breeze to the countless scents flooding my nostrils that I hadn't noticed until that moment. I smelled pine needles, tree sap, and dead leaves - but there was something else too. I paused my panic for a second, trying to control my breathing, and breathed in deep. It almost smelled like...*smoke!* My heart jolted as my mind raced with possible scenarios that would cause smoke to be in the air from forest fires to barbecues.

Ruling out the latter, I got nervous about the possibility of the former. Without thinking, I worried that I had somehow set off a fire earlier, but I quickly realized I had no way of doing that and moved on to worry about the potential danger a fire would pose to me out there. While my mind jumped between worry and curiosity, I registered something specific about the fire, that it smelled sweet, like something was cooking. Now feeling less concerned about it being a wildfire, I gathered my bearings to figure out where it was coming from.

I slowly crept in the direction I could smell it, and soon I saw a faint glow through the trees. As I approached the source of the smoke, I thought I could hear voices but couldn't make out what was being said. I continued towards the glow and hoped with everything in me that I wasn't about to come upon a raging wall of fire. The closer I got, however, the more I was sure I was hearing voices, and not only that, but I thought they sounded familiar. I was agonizingly close to the source of the glow when I picked out the sound of laughter among the voices and realized I was hearing my own friends!

Confused, I jogged ahead through the trees and poked my head around a large oak tree to find a clearing with a campfire on the far side of it. Surrounding the fire was a large group of people that looked and sounded a lot like my friends from back home.

What were they doing here?

November

Into the Orchard

Caleb woke up early on Saturday morning to the sound of his parents stirring in the other rooms of the house. He grabbed his phone and saw, to his frustration, that it was just a couple of minutes before his alarm was going to go off. He stared at the ceiling for a second, thinking that he could have used those extra minutes of sleep, but he turned the alarm off instead and forced himself out of bed. As he got ready, he reoriented himself to reality, remembering what day it was. It was orchard day!

Caleb's family had always cared a lot about their routines and traditions, and that was especially true during Fall. Every year they went to a pumpkin patch, watched Halloween movies, and put up fall decorations around the house as soon as the first cool breeze drifted through in September. He enjoyed every moment of the season, but there was one tradition that held a special place in his heart: apple picking. He didn't love apples much more than the next guy, necessarily, but those cool mornings wandering through an old orchard were days he had come to rely on as each year brought new change for his family.

This year, there had been even more change than usual. For Caleb, junior year of high school had meant more challenging classes, trying to decide what he would do after graduation, and starting his first job. This was challenging enough as it was. What started as an easy, part-time gig that occupied a couple of night shifts a week became a grind that often bit into his weekends and kept him out late three or four nights a week instead. He liked the job itself well enough. Serving BBQ to locals really wasn't too bad in and of itself, but he was often worn out, and he had already missed some of the regular family time he usually looked forward to this time of year.

On top of this, Caleb's older brother had just recently moved out and started a new life several hours across the state. Now, instead of hanging out with Caleb at the local bookshop after school like they often did in the Fall, Blake was off starting graduate school in another city. He wouldn't have admitted it in so many words, but Caleb missed his brother. Over the Summer, when Blake first moved away, his absence hadn't set in fully with

Caleb, but as the coolness of the season began to settle in with September, nostalgia took over and brought up memories of years past that wouldn't be relived that year.

Despite the change that had rolled in with the new school year, though, Caleb had been enjoying Fall, just in a different way than usual. Trips to haunted houses and hayrides with friends had kept him occupied (when he could get away from work), but today was orchard day, and for the first time since they'd started going, Blake was going to miss it. As he finished getting ready and joined his parents in the living room, though, Caleb felt determined to enjoy the day anyway.

So, as he had in years past, Caleb found himself waking up earlier than he would have preferred on a Saturday morning and heading outside to hop in the minivan with his parents, vaguely thinking he should have grabbed something heavier to cover up as he walked out into the late Autumn air. The grass outside was covered in one of the first frosts of the year, as was the windshield. Caleb volunteered to scrape the thin layer of frost off, and he allowed the coolness of the morning to wake him up more. The sky was just now starting to become a light gray as the sun rose behind the clouds, and he hoped they would clear away as the morning progressed.

This year he was especially looking forward to this trip. If he was being honest with himself, he had been worried that it wouldn't happen with Blake being gone. Even with just one of them gone, Caleb had noticed a shift at home in their family dynamics.

Meanwhile, the two of them were beginning to have their own adventures as almost-empty-nesters. They had even gone on a camping trip by themselves a couple of months before on a weekend Caleb was working (which he was more than a little jealous about).

Despite all the change that was happening, though, there they were, in the van at 7:30 am on a Saturday, driving off to a nowhere-town that likely wouldn't appear on most maps. Caleb put in one of his headphones to listen to music as they drove, knowing it would be a while before they got to their destination, but he left one out to hear if his parents tried to get his attention.

The sun was coming up and lighting up everything, or so it seemed through the fog-covered windows. Caleb reached up to clear it away but hesitated and drew a pumpkin on the glass instead. *Very Fall-like,* he thought, admiring his handiwork for a second before scrubbing the rest of the condensation away to watch the outside world rush by as they drove.

With the heat now on full blast, his simple jacket kept him plenty warm. In fact, they had to turn the heat down now to keep from breaking out in a sweat. As they drove, Caleb got on his phone for a moment, but the anticipation of the day ahead distracted him, and he barely registered anything he was seeing. He was overwhelmed with the nostalgia he felt as they wound over backroads and under canopies of tree limbs overhead.

Just then, Caleb heard something his parents said that caught his attention, and he took out his earbud.

"What'd you say?" he asked.

"Blake just said he'll meet us there," his mom replied. "Where he lives now is about the same distance from the farm as us."

Caleb felt more excited at this than he would've admitted. He was surprised, not having considered that his brother would actually be able to join them. Maybe today wouldn't be so different after all!

Not wanting to betray his excitement, he simply responded by saying, "Oh, cool," and went back to looking out the window with his earbud in. For the next hour or so, he pondered what the day would now look like. He was glad Blake could join them, but he also wasn't quite sure what to expect from him. They'd talked off and on over the past several months, but it had been a long time since they had seen each other in person. How much could a few months of grad school change?

An hour or so later, they arrived at the small farm. It was a plain plot of land with what seemed like dozens of trees lined up in a field and a couple of wooden barns standing on one side of it. Looking out across the field, the dew was still shining bright in the early morning light. They pulled into the grass parking area where there were already a handful of cars that had arrived, and the three of them got out and walked towards the barn.

Caleb got his shoes quickly soaked as he walked through the wet grass. The minor inconvenience was an annoying but regular part of the yearly trip that came with the cool, Autumn morning. Caleb always told himself he'd try harder the next time to avoid getting his shoes wet, but that never seemed to happen. As they walked into the barn, Caleb threw one last glance over his shoulder towards the parking area to see if Blake's car had pulled up yet, but no new cars had appeared.

Stepping into the rustic barn, Caleb's nose was rushed by a thousand different scents from apple cider candles to damp leaves and the smell of old barnwood. There were a few families milling about on the hardwood floor, sending creaks and groans across the room. In the room they had entered were several items for sale like apple cider, shirts, and dish cloths with various fall patterns on them. Caleb's eyes darted from one item to the next, trying to decide if he'd brought enough cash to get anything. He saw his dad already inspecting the collection of apple ciders, scouting out what they would take home with them.

The next room had all sorts of baskets for gathering apples and a small fire pit that a few people were keeping warm around. Caleb wandered over to the fire and held out his hands to sap away the autumn chill that had seeped in since they left the van. The warmth was wonderful, but brief. His parents were soon gesturing him over to the baskets so they could go ahead and hunt down their bounty from the orchard.

The three grabbed their own baskets and made their way outside. Caleb let out his breath, watching the little clouds form in front of his face as he did, and was glad to be there again. He pondered for a moment how many of these trips they would do as a family. If he moved away after graduation, himself, he wasn't sure if they would all be back for apple picking in a couple years. At least they could get another year or two out of it in the meantime. Caleb glanced at the lot one more time as they moved toward the orchard. Still no Blake.

Apparently seeing the glance, Caleb's mom assured him Blake was on the way but had told them to go ahead and that he'd catch up. Satisfied with this answer, Caleb walked off on his own to explore the old grove of trees. Behind him, he heard the sounds of his mom's film camera as she grabbed a few shots of the orchard. Soon, he could no longer hear the faint *clicks* and was alone in his own world.

It was quiet among the trees, and all Caleb could hear was the sound of grass brushing aside where he walked and the occasional plunk of an apple hitting the bottom of his basket as he picked a few that hung on the lower branches. Meanwhile, he was searching the taller branches to see if any particularly large ones had been left higher up.

The orchard opened up once he got deeper in, and it was a lot bigger than it seemed from the outside. He thought at this point he would have known the orchard pretty well, but Caleb found himself lost after a few turns, and he couldn't quite tell where he was.

Despite the disorientation, he was in awe of the apple trees surrounding him. They were so tall and seemed unnaturally full for the time of year. They provided shade for the ground below, making it feel cooler than it was out in the sun. Between the leaves and branches, the sun poked through just enough to make light dance through the branches as they swayed in the breeze. Caleb turned to look at each tree, scanning for any particularly big apples they might hold.

As he continued, he felt himself getting deeper into the orchard, and he, again, thought it seemed impossibly big. Most orchards they had gone to were pretty small and, honestly, a little sparse, but this almost seemed more like a small forest.

Occasionally he thought he heard a voice echo through the trees, but otherwise, it was silent. Suddenly the orchard opened up into a small clearing. In the center, the sun shone on the ground, uninterrupted by trees overhead. There, the grass was already dry from dew that had soaked Caleb's socks earlier.

He stood in the middle of the clearing for a moment, soaking in the sun, feeling it get a little warmer as it rose higher in the sky. A gentle breeze ran through the trees around him, and a feeling of peace washed over him. Absentmindedly, Caleb set his basket down with the few apples he'd already picked, and he laid down in the grass. He let himself relax for a second, nearly dozing off in the sun.

Suddenly, Caleb heard a rustling as someone came into the clearing, and he bolted up to see who it was.

"I'm, what, ten minutes late, and you're already falling asleep on the job?" Blake grinned as he strolled into the clearing with all the pomp that an older brother could have after being away.

Caleb laughed and hopped up quickly, "I was just giving you a fighting chance. Or did you think we weren't competing this year just because you can't get out of bed on time?"

Every year the two of them competed to see who could find the biggest, juiciest apple in the orchard. For years they had traded wins back and forth, but Caleb was on a two-year winning streak, and he didn't pass up a chance to rub that in Blake's face, of course.

"Oh, I see," Blake said, his voice dripping with sarcasm, "This is mercy, huh? Well, thank you so, so much."

With that he gestured to the trees around them. "Well, what are we waiting for?"

The two of them walked off, now both paying extra attention to the higher branches where there would still be apples that hadn't been taken yet.

"So, did you miss me?" Blake asked, bumping him from the side.

"I didn't miss the space you take up. I have much more room now."

His older brother returned Caleb's smile and laughed as they continued to talk and walk between the trees. He never let on directly, but Caleb had missed his brother's presence at home. It was...different now. It was true he had more room, but he sometimes found himself missing his roommate.

As they continued their search, though, Caleb was reassured that things weren't quite so different, after all. Blake talked to him about his new life in grad school, relaying some of the interesting stories he had from the past several months of new friends and a local bookshop he had explored.

"Don't worry, I haven't forgotten about Red Dragon," he said, referring to the local bookshop they'd spent so much time in before. "This place is cool, but I do miss our old stomping grounds."

Unsurprisingly, Blake maintained his typical, cool demeanor, but Caleb knew him well enough to pick up on the subtle signs that the move had been difficult on him, too. Even just in the way he mentioned their favorite bookstore told Caleb that he missed home. In a weird way, it comforted Caleb to know that the change was challenging for Blake, too. He was glad Blake hadn't completely moved on from his old life just yet.

Of course, the brothers weren't going to let the conversation completely distract them from the task at hand, and soon, Caleb spotted just the right apple, high above them.

"That's a winner for sure," Caleb muttered to himself, seeing the bright, big orb near the top of a tree nearby.

The tree that held their prize seemed to be an older one, much older than many of the others. It was wide and had strong, thick branches that stretched higher than the ones around it.

Caleb immediately regretted saying anything, seeing that Blake had heard him. He smirked at Caleb, challenging him for the prize, and of course, Caleb would not back down.

The two brothers raced off for the trunk, and dropping their baskets, both leapt up to the lower branches and climbed. Carefully, but quickly, they raced through the tree, each taking different routes to the apple. Before they could get there, though, Caleb was drawn away by a splash of bright yellow that was peeking out of the tree. Doubling back for just a moment, he found that the color was coming from an opening in the trunk.

Inside, Caleb saw the space was filled with honey! He moved to the next branch over to get a closer look. Apparently bees had made their home inside the opening, and they had constructed honeycombs full of the golden liquid. The sun was at just the right angle so that the honey was shining brightly. Caleb thought it was abandoned for a second, but then he saw the bees drift into the sunlight from the darker corners of the makeshift hive.

Instinctively, he jolted back on the branch he stood on, but the bees didn't seem to pay him any attention. They buzzed lazily back and forth between the honeycombs, hardly acknowledging the newcomer at all. A couple of curious ones drifted out and landed on the branch Caleb was hanging on to, causing him to shift back, trying to be slow so he didn't provoke them. He stopped moving when they got closer, hoping they wouldn't sting him. One landed gently on his hand, inspected it for a second, and gave Caleb a quick glance before going back and joining the others.

I guess I passed, Caleb thought. The bees drifted back into the opening and continued what they were doing. Caleb found himself mesmerized by the movement, now that the immediate threat of harm was gone. He thought it was amazing how the little community had taken up residence inside the tree and seemed to be thriving peacefully. He probably would've stayed there watching longer, but just then, he heard a call from above, grabbing his attention.

His brother had beaten him to the apple! Caleb sighed to himself, mildly frustrated at his own curiosity. He took one last look at the bees where they seemed to be watching him cheerfully. It felt sort of silly, but he waved to them before leaving and climbed down to the once again. Caleb carefully dropped from the lower branches to the ground where Blake was already leaning against the tree, gloating.

"Good effort, though, really," his brother said, laughing as he tossed the apple up to himself and catching it with an obnoxious flourish. He dropped it in his basket with a loud *thunk* and extended his hand to shake Caleb's.

"Good game."

Caleb was slightly annoyed at the loss, but he shook Blake's hand, laughed it off and told Blake about the strange colony of bees he'd come across.

"Pacifist bees?" Blake said, incredulously. "That's a new one. Cool, though."

They continued their search through the orchard, talking about past experiences with bees and how they wished more bee had the orchard ones' gentle disposition. The sun had risen higher above the trees at that point, making the November morning feel warmer than expected. The two brothers walked along for a few minutes, silently scanning the trees around them, before Blake interrupted the quiet.

"Honestly," he said, "this has been really nice. I'm...really glad I was able to make it back for this."

Something about the way he said that confirmed what Caleb had thought earlier. The stories Blake had brought back from graduate school had Blake's natural sense of adventure woven into them, but it seemed that the move had been challenging for him, too. He specifically told Caleb that being able to meet up with them, even for just the morning, helped him feel a little more grounded.

Caleb thought about how the transition had been for him and was glad for the moment of frankness with his brother as they talked about the weirdness that came with change. Caleb returned the honesty and expressed how he truly had missed Blake being around. This seemed to lift Blake's spirits a little, and Caleb began to feel better, too. He thought about the consistency of family and peaceful bees that lived in trees.

They spent the next half hour or so looking through tree branches to find good apples for home, and they managed to find several more that were large, though none quite so big as the one they had found earlier. It felt like it was too soon, but they eventually noticed that the sun had come to rest directly overhead, and their stomachs confirmed that it was nearly lunchtime. The brothers wound their way out of the orchard, and Caleb realized it felt less overwhelming going out than it had going in. Navigating it felt much more manageable, now.

When they met up with their parents, again, everyone compared their hauls as they walked back to the barn to check out. Inside, the fire was no longer quite as necessary as the sun warmed everyone. They grabbed a couple jugs of apple cider along with the apples and called it a day.

Beside the barn was a small cafe that had an empty table perfect for four, so they each grabbed a seat and ordered the greasiest thing they could find on the menu to revive them after the long morning hunting apples. The food was perfect, and the cafe felt cozy as more families joined them inside after spending the morning wandering through the vast orchard.

As they ate, Blake told their parents some of his stories from the past few months that he had already recounted to Caleb, ending, of course, with a dramatization of his victory to reach the apple in the tree from earlier. Caleb playfully refuted some of the more exaggerated details but let him have his victory, promising there would be a different result next year.

"So, you all want to keep doing this, then?" their dad asked. "I know this isn't the easiest thing to coordinate with grad school and jobs-"

Before he could fully get the sentence out, Caleb and Blake enthusiastically insisted on continuing their Autumn ritual. Caleb could tell their parents were relieved they wanted to keep it going, and for a moment, he felt especially close with his family.

Too soon, though, lunch was finished, and it was time to leave. Their mom, of course, insisted on taking their usual family photo, this time with her new/old film camera, and for the first time in years, the brothers didn't object at all. She had set the camera up on a nearby railing when someone nearby offered to take it for them, though that proved to be an adventure since they needed instruction on how to use the vintage camera. After a brief tutorial, they got the camera focused on Caleb and his family and said, "Cheese!"

Click

They frowned and looked at the back of the camera as if to check how the photo turned out.

"Uh, is that it?"

"Yes, that's perfect!" Caleb's mom said, reaching out for the camera, starting her spiel about how cool film photography was.

Blake chuckled a little under his breath and whispered to Caleb, "I see Mom's enjoying her new hobby."

"Yes, that is definitely true. I hope all these photos actually turn out well when she gets them developed," Caleb whispered back.

"That would be really tough if she finds out half of them were taken with the lens cap on or something."

The two of them snickered quietly at the thought, and overhearing them, their dad said, "Hey, her last pictures turned out perfect, thank you," but he chuckled a little, too. It was a small thing, but it felt very normal for Caleb. Some things never change.

It was starting to get late into the afternoon by then, so they finally went back to where they'd parked their cars in the grass lot. Blake gave hugs to everyone and promised he would see them soon for Thanksgiving, and with that, he got in his car and headed back to his new home. Caleb and his parents piled into their van with their bags of apples and jugs of apple cider and started the journey home as well.

Caleb dozed off on the drive, his tiredness catching up with him from the work week before, but when they arrived at home he hopped up to help unload everything. As usual, they had brought home way more than they would need, so they divided them up to give the extras to Caleb and Blake's grandparents and some of their neighbors.

Later that evening, Caleb had retreated to his room to wind down, and he had just decided against calling Blake to catch up more when Blake actually called him! He quickly answered the phone, and they launched into a conversation that would keep them up for another couple of hours before calling it for the night.

They promised to catch up again soon, and Blake told Caleb he needed to visit sometime, to which Caleb agreed. When they hung up, Caleb took a deep breath and let out some of the anxiety that had been sitting in his chest. *Everything was going to be ok.*

That night Caleb fell asleep feeling content that his family wasn't so different now, after all, and a couple weeks later, after it had been developed, they had a perfect picture to prove it.

Wandering alone, in the dark
You will quickly lose your way

Where the bee stings, wind bites
And skeleton trees stretch into the sky

But high in the trees of the Forest
Gold freely flows and sweet fruit grows

And loneliness has no place there

- C.E.

Coffee and Vines

Cassie opened her eyes to see sunlight streaming in through her bedroom window. She bolted upright, her heart already racing, and she fumbled with her phone to see what time it was. Already *8:30! Why didn't the alarm go off?!*

She swung her legs out of bed to start getting ready when she realized what day it was. Her mind was struggling to reset as she remembered it was Saturday, and she hadn't set an alarm the night before because, for once, she didn't need one. She rubbed her eyes for a second and sighed. Sleeping in was easier said than done sometimes. She rolled back over and tried to go back to sleep for a few minutes.

Cassie was tired. Her and her husband, Charlie, had not been in their new house for very long when things started to go wrong. She often found herself wondering if the move had been worth it, after all. They had originally decided to leave their old house because it was, well, old. It would have needed a lot of work to get it in good shape, and frankly, they didn't have the time or money to invest in that sort of project. She and Charlie had kept an eye out for an opportunity to move, so when their realtor reached out with a house she thought they'd like, they were ready to go all in. Now that their two oldest daughters were out of the house, it was a good time for a change.

Unfortunately, the new house had ended up being a bit of a nightmare. Cassie's husband usually avoided such strong language - ever the optimist - but Cassie felt it was appropriate with all the little "projects" that had sprung up since they'd moved in. The joys of homeownership were limitless. Shingles fell off the roof, drains quit working, and, for a few days, the heat was out! It seemed like an unending trail of work that made them miss the ease of apartment life when a maintenance crew would fix those sorts of things.

It didn't help that a lot of change had been happening at work for Cassie. She was an elementary school teacher, which was chaotic enough as it is, but this year there was a huge curriculum change that messed with the majority of the lesson plans she had crafted over the years. Needless to say, it was taking some adjustment to retool everything to the new standards. More than she had in a long time, this year she had to create a lot of her lesson plans from scratch, and that meant long hours planning. On top of the move, that left very little free time.

Now it was November, and they'd been in the house for about 6 months without a break to really enjoy it. While she was lesson planning and taking care of Ben, Charlie had his own share of working late nights throughout October to keep up with the busy season at his job. Between the two of them, it seemed like one of them was always working or fixing whatever was wrong with the house that day. Fortunately, Charlie's job slowed down when November hit, but Cassie was still in desperate need of a break.

Fall was usually her favorite season, but between lesson planning, housework, and helping Ben adjust to a new home, Cassie was worn out. It didn't help that they hadn't really been able to decorate much for the season this year. Blank walls stared at her every day when she walked through the house, mocking her for her apathy and for not digging out the decoration box yet. If it weren't for the fresh roses Charlie had brought home recently, the house would be completely dreary. Cassie just felt like she needed a moment to breathe.

At the end of the second week in November, Charlie could tell Cassie was burnt out and decided to try and help. They had originally planned to take Ben to his friend's birthday party together on Saturday, but Charlie knew Cassie needed that time to herself, so he told her he'd take Ben, and she could spend that morning relaxing. Cassie was grateful for her husband, who, as always, knew just what she needed - and knew she wouldn't have asked for that herself. Now having the morning to relax, she took the chance to call up one of her friends to meet her for coffee.

Now, Cassie laid in bed trying to go back to sleep, but unfortunately she was wired to be up early. Defeated, she crawled out from the warm covers after lying in bed for another half hour, and she made her way to the living room. Out of habit, she started to grab a mug for her morning coffee when she remembered that she had in fact called her friend Bianca to meet up for coffee later that morning at a nearby shop that Cassie hadn't checked out yet. Not used to having so much time to spare, she wasn't sure what to do in the meantime. Normally in her free time she would continue working on another project the house had thrown at them, but Charlie had insisted she didn't work on the house at all that weekend.

Cassie found herself in the office pursuing the bookshelf they had set up the week before. They hadn't filled it yet, but there were a few books sitting on the top shelf. She reached for one she hadn't read before and took it back to the couch in the living room.

It had been months since she had actually read a book for fun, and it was almost difficult to get back into the right mindset to absorb the words on the page in front of her. She tried for a chapter or so before giving up. Her mind could not focus on the story, and it was nearly time to get ready for the day anyway. She left the book on the coffee table, already prepared to break her own empty promise to come back to it later.

She spent the next half hour or so getting dressed in a comfy outfit, brushing her teeth, and generally making herself feel like a real person before braving the outside world. She enjoyed the luxury of taking a leisurely pace to get ready, as she typically had to cram the process into a 15-minute window before rushing out the door to work or church or any number of events that always seemed to fill their schedule.

Although it felt unnatural, she savored the rare opportunity to not rush through the morning. When she was ready, with plenty of time to get to the coffee shop, she stepped out into the world. The shop was just over a mile from their house, right outside the neighborhood, so she took the sidewalk.

It was a cool, cloudy November morning that begged for a hot latte and a warm sweater. Cassie was looking forward to the warmth she imagined awaited her inside the small shop, but she also enjoyed the cool stillness of the day. She could see small clouds form in front of her as she breathed, and she was glad she'd put on her homemade beanie. It wasn't the kind of thing she would wear to the office, but she was glad for the excuse to get it out. It made the day feel a little more comfortable for her to be in.

The walk was peaceful, despite the noise of her mind still rattling through her to-do list. Old habits die hard. Occasionally, the cold wind would blow sharply and interrupt her thoughts, making her shiver. In some ways, though, the coolness of the morning made her feel more alive than she had in weeks. By the time she arrived at the Dragonfly Coffeehouse, her nose was slightly red from the cold breeze, and she was thankful to duck into the warmth of coffee-scented air.

The wood floor creaked just slightly as she walked up to the counter, the smell of coffee and tea flooding her senses. As she ordered, she realized how long it had been since she drank coffee for any reason other than getting her caffeine fix to get her through the day. For the first time in weeks, she decided to add some fun flavoring to her latte that she normally wouldn't spring for.

The scene inside the shop almost felt like it had been crafted just to relax Cassie. The dull murmur of clinking mugs and conversation worked together in harmony with the espresso machine whirring behind the counter, and the lighting was soft and warm. Outside the window by the counter, light gray clouds filled the sky but still let sunlight filter through. The last of the November leaves were shaking in the breeze on the branches of the large maple tree that sat next to the shop.

The cozy shop sat on a side street, a little removed from the traffic of the main highway, and it was in an old house that was probably over 50 years old and had a sign that said "The

Dragonfly" hanging above the door that was probably as old as the house itself from a past business that resided there. Having lived on the other side of town for years, Cassie hadn't made it past her usual spot for a coffee fix near their old house to pop into this one before, but she felt strangely at home there.

When her name was called, she retrieved her coffee and began a slow search of the rooms to see if Bianca had already made it there. The walls were covered in paintings from local artists and leafy designs that made you feel like you were walking amongst trees, and Cassie's coffee warmed her hands as she explored the house. Each room she went through was unique while also maintaining the same vibe of the one before it, and Cassie slowly went through them one-by-one, examining the local art as she went.

She found Bianca in a side room at a small table with comfy seats and sank into the nearest chair. The room was illuminated with soft light from the windows, and an old fireplace made of dull, red bricks was positioned on the wall next the table they were at.

Even though the two of them hadn't actually spoken in weeks, it was like no time had passed at all as they began joking with each other about the sweaters they were wearing that were who knows how old now. Cassie thought about when they bought the sweaters at a thrift shop together in college, missing how simple things were then. By the time their coffee had cooled down enough to drink, they had already settled back into a natural rhythm that never seemed to go away no matter how long it went before they saw each other.

Cassie felt her back relax and her jaw unclench (had it been tight that whole time?) as they caught up on the stories from the past several months and laughed at weeks-old jokes. Her latte warmed her as she sipped it, and the scent of vanilla surrounded her. At one point she found herself just taking in the fall decor around her. Red and yellow plastic leaves were draped over the fireplace mantle and should've looked cheap, but they made the room feel cozy. She looked at the Autumn-themed paintings that covered the walls and thought of her own that were hidden in boxes somewhere.

"I never did end up really decorating for Fall like I wanted to," she sighed.

Bianca made a face, clearly saying she did not believe that for a second, but Cassie insisted, "It's true! I know I always say that, but I *really* didn't this year. With this move...everything's just been so busy."

"That is so unlike you," Bianca said, now seeming a little concerned.

"I know, but it's been so busy. I don't know where the decorations even are at this point."

"You could always grab some cheap ones from a thrift shop or something, just in the meantime." Bianca said.

"Oh, when would I even go do that?"

"What are you doing now?"

"Now? Oh, well-"

"Great! Let's finish these drinks and head over!"

Before Cassie could think of an excuse, she found herself downing the rest of her latte and being rushed out the door.

Bianca said the store wasn't very far from the coffee shop, so the two of them walked down the sidewalk the half mile or so between the two places. The clouds kept the sun from warming much of anything, so Cassie pulled out a beanie and placed it carefully on her head. She and Bianca crunched rust-colored leaves beneath their feet that were left over from the leaf blowers that had come through that morning, and they continued talking about everything else in life they may not have covered yet.

The soft sunlight pushed through the clouds and lit up the small shops that had cropped up beside the sidewalk. This corner of town had a lot of fun boutiques and shops that the locals loved. Cassie noticed "Shop Local!" and "Support Small Businesses" signs and wondered who ran these places. They hadn't moved very far - just across town - but she was unfamiliar with this area and was constantly reminded of it. She shook her thoughts away and locked back in on what Bianca was saying.

"I'm so glad you're on this side of town now! I love it over here. And the shops are just the best! This thrift store we're going to has some of the best deals and the CUTEST decorations!"

Cassie nodded politely but was feeling stressed thinking about sifting through dusty decorations and putting them up at home. She was starting to think she'd rather just wait until Christmas and hopefully try decorating for that. Bianca, however, was persistently enthusiastic that morning.

Soon, they were in the small thrift store, rifling through discount bins that were full of fall decor that others had overlooked for the bright Christmas decorations.

"Oh, I shouldn't even bother. Christmas will be here before we know it, and I'll have to take all this down anyway," Cassie said, also feeling overwhelmed at the prospect of decorating a Christmas tree, too.

"No, no, no. We do NOT overlook Autumn. Come on, now, let's find something you like," Bianca insisted.

It took a few minutes, but Cassie slowly got more excited as she found a few crocheted pumpkins that she, admittedly, thought were really cute. She found a few good strands of oversaturated red and orange leaves to drape over the mantle and even a couple old, fall pictures that showed full, colorful trees and old farm equipment. One had a John Deere tractor that reminded her of the one her granddad used to ride around the garden when she was growing up. She grabbed it along with the other decorations and paid the $30 dollars or so they all cost.

Feeling better, she accepted Bianca's offer to come over and put it all up with her. Bianca had driven to the coffeehouse, so she drove them both back. At the house, they began covering shelves in fake leaves and placing the pumpkins on tables. The Fall pictures and paintings went up, and a couple candles were lit to cap off the ambience.

As they worked, they put on a record that recalled images of forests and lakes wrapped in cool weather. The needle exposed soft notes hidden in the grooves of the vinyl, and the speaker crackled out an old voice wishing summer goodbye and embracing an autumn moon. The music went through the house and wound through newly placed decor.

Cassie felt her energy levels rising and even took the time to search through a few of her unpacked boxes and found some of the other fall decorations (though she had a lot more still somewhere in that house). The scent of pumpkin and pine-scented candles transformed the house into their own cozy oasis sitting in the middle of an autumn forest. The rug became a layer of lush grass covering the ground they walked on, candles became fireflies that danced in spite of the cooler weather, and couches became large, moss-covered logs that the two friends could relax on between opening boxes. The tiny flames in the candles joined the leaves in a dance that was timed to the gentle melody spilling from the record player. Cassie finally smiling wide and laughing freely with Bianca.

Once the inside was properly decorated, they opened the door to let their oasis grow onto the porch. Pumpkins and wreaths tumbled out of their autumn forest and made themselves at home on hooks and by doorposts outside.

Cassie noticed a vine had crept its way onto the porch railing. It was a muted green and looked strong. It almost seemed to hold the porch railing itself together. A couple small orange and yellow blooms peeked out of the green, which Cassie thought was odd. It took a moment, but she recognized the flower. *Pumpkins,* she realized. *It's a little late for them to be flowering now, isn't it? How did they survive the frost?*

She inspected it closer, trying to decide if she would remove it. The fact that it was flowering at this point of the year was unusual, and she couldn't imagine it would survive much longer with the coming Winter. Still, she hated to get rid of the bright flowers.

The vine waited expectantly, apparently content with whatever she decided. She almost pulled it from the railing but decided against it. Instead, she reached out and gently plucked off one of the blooms and brought it inside to add to a bouquet of roses Charlie had recently placed on the mantle. She thought it'd be a fun splash of new color among the deep reds and pinks.

The vine graciously gave her its brightest flower. Bianca, of course, was extremely enthusiastic about the find and asked if she could take a couple small blooms as well. Cassie didn't mind, and the vine granted her request.

Back inside, they felt how the autumn breeze had chilled their fingers and noses, and they were thankful for the warm house that now felt a little more like home. Bianca regretfully told Cassie she would have to leave, but the look on her face expressed her satisfaction with the afternoon.

Cassie thanked her friend for the warmth she brought into the Autumn morning and for all the help, and they promised they would get together more often. With that, Bianca exited into the cool afternoon air. Now alone in the house, Cassie breathed in the fall scents from the candles and curled up on the couch. She took another shot at reading her book and found it much easier than earlier that day.

When Charlie returned with Ben later that afternoon, they were ecstatic about the new decor!

"And to think we'd given up on getting the house decorated this year. It looks so good!" Charlie said as they examined the thrift store finds. "Thank you, my love."

Cassie brushed off the thanks, saying it was really for her anyway. Among the soft colors and subtle pumpkin scent, she felt better than she had in weeks. Time with a friend and settling her home for the remainder of the Autumn season had already made a huge difference to her stress levels.

Cassie's knee-jerk response had been to avoid it, but she was so glad that she let herself get talked into decorating with her friend. *Thank goodness for Bianca's natural stubbornness and undying support,* she thought to herself.

Now with her family for the evening, Cassie felt at home, or she at least felt much more at home than she had before. Fall was always a time of celebrating and cozying in, and she finally felt it as Charlie got a fire going in the fireplace and put on a cozy movie. It wasn't perfectly settled yet, but the house was a little closer to what she had been hoping for. As they watched the movie, Cassie relaxed and sipped some hot chocolate. She really was home.

The crackling of
A needle on vinyl
Like a heartbeat
Pumps life into a room

Slowly, peace floods in
Coating the walls with
Golden joy and the floor with
Soft, green moss

Time stands still
And breathes gently

The vine on the porch
Stops creeping for just a
Moment to enjoy the return of
Warmth and music

- C.E.

In the Forest

Sam had finished his Thanksgiving lunch and could feel the pull of a nap starting to set in. He cleaned off his plate and placed it in the dishwasher with the rest of his family's dishes, and as he walked back to the living room, he considered sinking into the recliner for a minute.

In the back of his mind, he felt the pull of his phone and the work emails that he could be sifting through. Glancing out the window at the late-fall day, though, he found a stronger pull coming from the bright, sunny afternoon sky. He willed himself to walk over to his brother, Leo, instead.

"Well, are we still going hiking?" he asked.

"Of course," Leo responded quickly, already jumping up. With that, the two of them put on their shoes and headed out the front door, letting a few people know where they were going. They invited their older brother, Oliver, to join, but he opted to stay inside.

Fair enough, Sam thought to himself as they stepped outside, *He probably doesn't want to leave Claire by herself on her first Thanksgiving.* Oliver had gotten married recently, and Sam could only imagine how nerve-wracking the first big holiday had been already. Still, he was sad for the break in tradition.

Outside, they felt how chilly the air had gotten. The late November sun felt warm on their faces but did not keep their extremities from starting to get cold. They descended the wooden porch stairs, causing them to creak with each step, and went over to Sam's car where he had stashed several jackets, hats, and other gear to help them stay warmer while they were out.

He picked out a warm sweatshirt and a beanie to pull onto his head, and he switched out his tennis shoes for hiking boots. Leo grabbed a hat but, otherwise, said he didn't need anything else. Sam shot him a skeptical look but didn't push it. The car door thudded as it closed, and the two brothers marched off on their regular route to the beginning of the old path in the woods.

Every year after Thanksgiving lunch, the two of them (usually with Oliver) had made a tradition of trekking through the forest that pushed up against their grandparents' backyard.

After a while, jobs and school prevented them from visiting as often as they used to outside of the holidays, so these little expeditions became their way of checking in to see what growth had sprung up in the year before. Sam hadn't been sure if they would actually go this year with all the life changes, but it seemed like Leo was as determined as he was to keep the tradition going, despite the cool demeanor he put on.

Leo was now in high school and liked for others to treat him like an adult, but it seemed like he wasn't too cool yet to keep for their annual hike, at least for one more year. Sam couldn't help but smile as they approached the worn-out path that they had walked down so many times before. They had found the entrance when they were all younger and thought it was a mystical path that had opened up just for them like something out of the Narnia books.

Although they knew it was likely just a path deer had carved out, they still felt a sense of wonder as they walked up to it. As they got closer to the tree line, they avoided stepping on leaves so as to keep their presence a secret from the creatures inside for a little longer. They stopped a few feet away from the gap in the trees and took in their surroundings.

The sun had sunk just below the tops of the trees from the angle they were looking at, and its light filtered through the branches and few remaining leaves. They listened intently and could hear small chirps from birds darting into the woods and leaves crunching as squirrels hopped around. When the breeze picked up, the gusts of wind whistled through hollowed out logs that sat somewhere in the thick forest ahead. The air was just cold enough for their breath to show in small clouds. Without a word, Sam led the way through the opening, ducking slightly he slipped into another world.

Leo fell in behind him and immediately pointed out a couple trees that seemed to have doubled in size since they last saw them, and Sam noted a couple spots where deer had pushed through the undergrowth to create their new trails. They walked carefully over the damp leaves, trying to avoid making noise as they slipped between the trees around them. The path wound back and forth in a familiar pattern, and Sam and Leo quietly pointed out little things they saw to each other that could only be noticed when you walked slowly and silently.

A new bird's nest cradled in a high crook of a tall tree.

A rabbit, darting through the undergrowth nearby.

A scraped-up tree from a deer that had gone through.

An imprint in the earth left by wandering turkeys.

Sam then recognized an old, mostly-dead tree that signaled their proximity to the creek that ran through nearby. Leo also noticed it and brushed his hand over the bark as they passed by. From there, they could hear the sound of running water, and after dodging through a thicket of vines and brambles, they saw the wide, deep creek. The dark water rushed gently over rocks and past the trees that stood guard in walls on each bank. Sam and Leo walked along, picking up rocks and seeing who could skip them the farthest. Occasionally they'd find a particularly unique rock and stash it in a pocket somewhere.

As they walked, the two brothers began to talk more freely as the rushing sound of water broke the silence of the forest for them. Leo talked about the challenges of high school to his older brother, mentioning some of the harder classes he'd had to deal with and the new levels of drama that swirled through his friend group. Leo had also started his first job at the hardware store and was finding that working life wasn't all it was cracked up to be. Sam nodded knowingly and offered a couple small pieces of advice, when asked for. Hearing about high school and part-time jobs almost made him miss the comparative simplicity of that age.

Sam once again thought of the work emails piling up in his email inbox. Being fresh out of college, he had felt the pressure to excel in his new job, and it often became a constant stressor, even during the holidays. Based on what Leo was saying, it sounded like he was feeling the anxiety of having to constantly be working, and in his case, studying, too. Sam thought to mention his own challenges but thought better of it. He was happy to just listen for now.

As the two of them walked, they left the creek and crept along the edge of a large hill that dropped down to their right. Occasionally, one of them would kick a rock over the edge to watch it pick up speed before crashing into a tree at the bottom.

The brothers avoided getting too close to the edge, though. Leo was speaking freely, now, walking through the stress he'd felt with the new school year and the struggle to balance work hours and homework.

"You know what, though?" he said, after several minutes of talking it all through, "I think I am getting the hang of it all, though. I just have to keep remembering that there's more to life than the constant grind and trying to get ahead. Really, doing things like this is really helpful. I feel more focused on real life out here."

Sam nodded, astounded at the wisdom his brother had spoken.

"I wish I had more of your perspective," he said, thoughtfully.

"What do you mean?"

"Well, adjusting to adult life has been a little harder than I expected. I have a hard time balancing work with, well, 'real life.'" Sam replied, trying not to take too much of the focus of the conversation.

"Sam," Leo said, stopping. "Are you alright?"

"Oh, I'm fi-" Sam was cut off by a loose root that snagged his foot, sending him forward and to the right, down the hill they'd been avoiding.

He tumbled through leaves and over roots sticking out of the hill, picking up bumps and bruises along the way before finally stopping at the bottom, narrowly missing a large tree nearby. Leo stood frozen at the top of the hill, still registering what had happened. Suddenly what he had seen caught up with his body, and he sprang into action.

"Sam!" he yelled, now carefully sliding down the hill, trying not to stand up all the way to avoid tumbling down himself. Down below, Sam stirred slowly and pushed himself to a sitting position. Leo hurried to get down, worried about his older brother, when he heard that Sam was laughing!

"What are you laughing about, you maniac?" Leo shouted, now sliding the last few feet and catching his momentum on a tree.

Sam laughed louder, "That was awesome! I almost want to do it again."

Leo rolled his eyes and shook his head, but Sam kept laughing. When he composed himself, he took quick stock of his injuries and everything seemed to be in one piece.

"Barely a scratch," he confirmed, patting himself down.

"You got lucky," Leo said, hiding his relief.

"Well, I'll take luck over skill any day..."

Sam dropped the thought, now looking ahead, away from the hill behind them. Just a few yards into the forest, he noticed a splash of color under a tree. Leo followed his gaze and saw what had caught his attention. Together, they walked towards it and, upon closer examination, they saw it was a pumpkin! And not just one but several of them, all growing from winding, green vines near the root of the old, maple tree that stood there.

"That's odd," Leo noted. "Have you ever seen pumpkins growing out here like this?"

Sam shook his head. "I didn't think pumpkins *could* grow out here like this."

Sam was baffled at the newest member of the forest growth. Pumpkins, to his understanding, did not typically just spring up in the woods. In fact, he hadn't ever seen one grow up naturally. Yet, here they were, growing right in the middle of the forest. In fact, the pumpkins looked very at home in the shade of the maple tree, and they almost seemed to invite the two of them to stop and stay for a while. The late sun splashed the scene in a soft glow that made Sam feel very at peace.

"How about we sit?" he suggested.

The brothers sat against the old tree, next to the pumpkins, and watched the woods as the sunlight filtered through the tree trunks. As they sat, Sam admired the bright pumpkin next to him that had seemingly popped up out of nowhere, apparently thriving in the most unlikely of places. It watched over them with a quiet, calming wisdom. As they sat, the cool air and warm light brought a peace that quieted Sam's mind for just a moment.

He glanced over at Leo and saw that he had pulled out his pocketknife and was quietly whittling a stick he'd picked up.

Sam again thought of the "real life" Leo had mentioned. The thought challenged him. *How do I find that?* He wondered.

Suddenly a bird swooped overhead and landed on a branch above them. It chirped a bright tune that wound through the trees and drew everything in closer. The pumpkins beside Sam listened quietly. Everything sat still, except the birds that came to the call and joined their friend on the tree branch. Sam watched them thoughtfully.

The sunlight was starting to dim slightly through the leaves overhead, and they continued their silence to watch as deer wandered the woods and squirrels hopped from one tree to the next. Sam enjoyed seeing how easily the deer would climb up or down the hill, barely disturbing the leaves as they went. Occasionally one would come a little closer to where the two brothers were seated and give them a suspicious glance before trotting off again.

Wait, he thought, *real life is right here, isn't it?* As he did every year, Sam marveled at the life around him and how it all seemed to happen right under his nose when he wasn't paying attention. Somehow, when he was only focused on passing through, it was easy to miss everything that was happening right in front of him. *Were the leaves always so vibrant? Were the trees always so breathtaking?*

Out of the corner of his eye, he saw Leo looking around at the Forest, too. He nodded slowly, as if to answer Sam's unsaid question. *This is real life, and it's happening all around us.* Sam felt his body relax into the mossy tree trunk. *I've missed this so much,* he thought.

As the sun set further, the cool breeze became much cooler. Leo sheepishly mentioned that he was getting colder than he expected, despite deciding to leave his coat behind earlier. Sam chuckled quietly and gave Leo his extra to keep warm. It wasn't long before the sun was almost completely hidden by the tree around them, so they decided it was a good time to head back.

Before they walked away, Sam took another look at the mini pumpkin patch that had made itself at home under the old tree. Amazed that no animals had eaten them yet, Sam decided to maneuver a few branches around the gourds to protect them for a little longer. With luck, maybe they would find more pumpkins the next year.

They quickly, but carefully, climbed the big hill and raced back through the forest, trying to beat the fading light back to the old log cabin. Their stomachs were starting to grumble, reminding them of the Thanksgiving leftovers that would be waiting for them when they returned, and the thought put an extra spring in their step as they wound back through the trees.

The trees were turning into dark silhouettes, now, but they didn't seem as scary as Sam would have thought. While they wove back through the forest on the path they'd taken in, the two of them saw shadows swooping above and heard loud cracks from the trees, but something about their visit this year shed a different light on it all. Instead of unknown dangers, Sam just saw sleepy owls coming out for the night and peaceful deer wandering to their beds. When he thought about the life around them, the dark forest seemed almost as magical as it did in the light.

Finally, they emerged from the opening in the woods where the trail began. The air outside was much cooler than before, but the stars were poking through the sky above, unprohibited by any sort of light pollution out there. Just as darkness fully settled in, they arrived at the wooden porch. The windchimes that hung by the swing welcomed them with a gentle melody.

Sam felt the warm comfort of nostalgia as they climbed the creaky steps. He realized that real life had been choked out for him recently by the need to prove himself at work. Plus, between his new job, Oliver moving off and getting married, and Leo and Bailey growing up, he felt like change was constant right now in their family, but the consistency of a walk in the forest felt very grounding for him. He finally remembered again that real life was not so far away, if he stopped to look for it. He desperately hoped he could remember that when he went home later that week.

Inside, Sam could hear laughter, and his heart leapt as they approached the door, excited to join. He didn't even realize that he'd nearly forgotten about those work emails. They'd be there later. For now, he was ready to join the warmth of his family. He'd mess with Oliver a little for missing out on their walk and jump in on a game of cards with his cousins. Everything would undoubtedly feel right with the world, as it often did this time of year.

Sam didn't know how many more years their excursions would happen, traditions can't always last forever, after all, but he was so glad for this one. A little lighter and a little more at peace, the two brothers walked back into the warmth of the log house to join their family.

Thorns and thistles
Shoot up
Choke out
The light around us

But slowly, patiently
Birds in the attic
Kites in the sky
Pumpkins in the Forest

Push through the thorns
Pry off the briars
Bring warmth and relief
To our troubled souls

-C.E

Rest and Fruit Trees

"Well, look who it is!" I heard as I peeked out from behind a tree.

The scene before me was hard to process due to the sheer unlikelihood of it. Sure enough, it was a group of my friends gathered around a warm bonfire. Even from my spot at the tree line, I could feel the warmth radiate from the center of the clearing.

What an odd clearing it was, too. Glancing around, I noticed that this area of the forest didn't seem to follow the same rules as the one I had just been walking through. It was impossibly bright there, even aside from the bonfire. I could see every detail of the trees surrounding it, and nothing seemed to be obscured by shadows like you would expect at night.

The trees themselves also seemed like they came from a different forest entirely. They looked to have even more leaves on them than usual, glowing with warm reds and vibrant oranges in the firelight. The leaves themselves also looked impossibly large, almost like I could wear one as a shirt if I wanted. Surely that was a weird trick of the light, though, right?

Overhead, in the gap between the canopy of tree limbs, the clouds were sparser, and silver moonlight spilled through the spaces between the dark purple shapes. The wind seemed different, too. It wasn't so much a cold wind as a cool breeze (I hadn't even considered the difference before). I took all of this in quickly before my friends beckoned me over to the fire, again.

"What are you all doing here?"

A friend I recognized from church back home laughed and responded, "The better question is, where have you been?"

"I've been-" I started, but I shut my mouth, realizing I wasn't quite sure. "I- I guess I've been lost," I finally got out, looking at the expectant faces around me.

"Well, you're here now! Sit down for a minute. Relax," someone else said, gesturing to a wooden rocking chair nearby.

I made my way to the seat and sank into the soft cushion that was tied onto it. Without thinking, I started pushing gently on the ground with my foot, causing the rocker to sway back and forth. I let out a sigh.

"That is better."

The bruises I had gotten from the tree branches felt like they had all but faded now, and the scrapes on my palms were nearly forgotten as the fire warmed my hands and feet. Now that I'd settled in, the dull buzz of conversation picked up between everyone again. My friends cycled through coming over and talking with me for what felt like hours, but I never got tired of talking with them and hearing about the adventures they'd had. It seemed like everyone had their own tale from the Forest and the journey they'd made to get through it, but somehow we all ended up there together.

I recounted my own adventures from my earlier walk in the Forest, and each person I told it to reacted perfectly to the ups and downs of the story. The more I told it, though, the more thankful I was for the warm fire and the peaceful oasis I'd stumbled into. Just as I was beginning to feel a little hungry, my friend, Jack, stood up on a log and called for everyone's attention.

"It's time for a feast!" he hollered over the crowd.

Everyone cheered and got busy moving chairs and tables together. Plates and cups and silverware seemed to just appear on the tables as everyone gathered around, and suddenly my family materialized from the tree line, carrying all sorts of food! They set it all on the table, and a few people gestured for me to come over. I sat down next to my parents, and some of my friends from college sat across from me.

Everyone began piling food onto their plates and passing baskets of rolls and bowls of mashed potatoes around to each other. I was overwhelmed with options and could hardly decide where to begin, but my mom offered to fix my plate, so I just sat back and enjoyed the scene of friends and family around me. As I started eating, I could really feel how hungry I had gotten. The food was so delicious and filling that it wasn't long before my stomach was contentedly full. It was then I turned to my parents and finally asked if they knew where we were.

My dad smiled at me, knowingly, and just said, "You're home." I must've looked skeptical because he continued.

"We know you've had a long trip. It's hard trying to find your way all by yourself, and you've been so brave. We also know you might get lost again one day - it's not always easy to stay in one place. But we want you to know that home is here, always waiting. Us and your friends are always here for you when you find your way back, and here you can rest and eat."

My mom reached over and squeezed my hand, and I felt my eyelids begin to droop as my body relaxed more.

"Oh, you must be tired. Come here, you can rest for a minute," she said, pulling me up from my seat and walking me over to a small cot on the edge of the clearing, near the fire. I climbed onto the cot and curled up under the blanket, feeling the fire warm me just enough without getting too hot.

"It's ok, you can rest now. It's been a long day, but it'll all be alright. Your dad and I have been right where you are before, and we know it can be exhausting. But you're safe here," my mom said. "We'll clean up and let you sleep."

With those words, I felt a profound sense of peace wash over me. I felt safe and comfortable, trusting my parents and friends to take care of me while I rested. As I drifted into a deep sleep, I was vaguely aware that the party had started cleaning up the leftovers from the feast. Then everything was black and quiet.

When I woke up, the clearing was emptier than it had been before. As I sat up and rubbed the sleep out of my eyes, I could see a handful of my friends hanging out in rocking chairs and sitting on logs around small fires that had been built in different spots of the clearing.

"Good morning, sleepyhead," I heard to my right. Turning, I saw it was my friend, Stan.

"Where is everyone?" I asked. My eyes were blinking hard while I tried to adjust to what seemed like morning like breaking through the trees.

Stan smiled, "Well, you didn't expect them to hang around forever, did you? Everyone has their own journey to go on."

I frowned at this. I was hoping they would stay for a while.

"Hey, don't worry," Stan assured me, "They'll all be back eventually. In the meantime, take it easy! There's no rush for you to get going again, so take as long as you need."

"Get going again?" I said. "To be honest, I was sorta hoping to stick around."

Stan sat down next to me. "You know, I understand that. A lot. But you'll move on, eventually. That's just life, I suppose. But what's so wonderful about this place is that once you find your way here, it's never really that far away. You can always find your way back, and we will be right here to help as you do." He stopped for just a moment before continuing.

"Besides, the Forest is never quite as bad when you leave." At this, he stood up and reached for a branch that hung low. He grabbed it, pulled something off, and tossed it over to me. I caught it and my eyes widened in surprise - *an apple!* I quickly looked up at the tree the branch came off of and saw that it was, in fact, a ginormous apple tree with dozens of apples hanging from it. *How did I not notice that before?* I gazed past the tree, past the tree line, into the forest that stretched out, away from the clearing, and I saw that many of the trees were full of wonderful fruit!

"See," Stan continued, "it's really a beautiful place. Sometimes it just takes the right people to help you see it."

With that, he wandered off again, leaving me with my thoughts and the apple he'd picked for me. I raised it to my lips and took a big bite. It was perfectly sweet.

Thanksgiving

Claire Emberly was finishing up her latest poem, signing it with her signature "C" at the bottom. She hesitated before adding the "E" next to it. She was still getting used to her new last name. C.E. Claire Emberly. She liked sharing a last name with Oliver, but it was an adjustment, regardless.

She stared at the poem she'd written, but after a moment reflecting on it, she scratched it all out with her pen and shut the journal. She just could not seem to get over her recent writer's block.

Her and Oliver had settled in on the loveseat a while ago after lunch wrapped up, and as some of the others were starting up games or watching football, the two of them were quietly sitting together, Oliver reading and Claire writing. Frustrated by her latest attempt at a poem, Claire sighed to herself and set her journal down on the floor.

It had been a long day for the two of them. As newlyweds, they were determined to make it to as many family festivities as possible, and fortunately their families lived close enough together to be there for both Thanksgivings. Unfortunately, they lived several hours away now, so that meant getting up early and driving over to get there in time for Claire's family Thanksgiving brunch.

They spent the first part of the afternoon catching up with her family, explaining in detail everything about their lives, and being fed platefuls of homemade food. It was a great time, but, of course, it was exhausting, too. Then around 2:00 they headed to Oliver's family Thanksgiving to do it all over again for an early dinner.

By this point, they had reexplained their jobs and reshared many of their stories from the past several months, and they had eaten more food until they were completely full. Now, they had moved to the loveseat to catch their breath for a moment and relax. Claire usually relaxed by writing out her feelings in poetry, but she couldn't get past the writer's block that had plagued her for the past few weeks. She felt a headache coming on just thinking about it.

Just then, Claire heard footsteps coming up onto the porch outside. She watched the two brothers step through the front door and let it swing shut behind them. Relieved, she found that their names popped easily into her head - Sam and Leo. At least she could keep Oliver's siblings straight. As for the rest of the family, though... She frowned to herself, thinking about how difficult it was to remember everyone's names. They had only been married a few months, but she felt obligated to remember it all, already. She glanced around the room again, silently quizzing herself.

The living room and adjacent dining room were full of family members playing games and talking to each other. Some were scattered on the couches and recliners, fighting sleep or reading books, while others were gathered at the table, starting to get into leftovers from lunch and playing a card game.

Claire scanned over each one, reciting the names she could remember to herself: *Charlie, Cassie, Grandpa Bill, Hannah, Caleb, Grandma Martha...* She was hitting her wall, though, which lit a spark of frustration that, combined with her already building exhaustion from the day, once again prompted a headache. She sat back on the couch with Oliver and resigned herself to at least running though the names she did know. She felt stress bubble up in her chest after a minute of this, so she instead decided to take in the house itself, again.

Fall decorations hung on shelves and sat on end tables, filling the room with splashes of orange, red, and yellow. Someone had put a fire on in the fireplace, and the golden flames were flooding the room with a pleasant warmth and soft light.

The smell of desserts baking and food being reheated swirled in the air.

One wall was made up of wood pieces that matched the outside log-cabin style build, while the other walls were painted a muted gray color. The colors all came together in a way that made the space feel open and cozy. Through the large window in the living room, Claire could see the last of the afternoon light fading.

The sunroom that branched off from the dining room was darker than before now that the sun had gone down, but an overhead light lit up the room and soft music from the radio inside it trickled into the living room over the murmur of voices that filled the house. The warmth of the cabin quelled Claire's anxiety, at least for a moment. She breathed in deep, held it, and let it out again slowly.

Meanwhile, the returning explorers kicked off their shoes by the door and re-greeted Grandpa Bill as he hurried over to hear what was new in the forest. Claire couldn't quite hear what they said, but Grandpa hung onto every word as they excitedly recounted their tales with hand gestures that she didn't understand from across the room.

A few family members overheard the exchange and laughed as they recounted their tales, but most of them were engrossed in a card game at the dining room table.

"Deal me in?" one of the brothers asked as he walked over to the table.

"Sure, but I'll warn you, your Grandma is running away with it, as usual," Uncle Charlie said with fake exasperation.

"I'll take my chances," Claire heard from around the corner.

The chatter increased, and Claire was feeling overwhelmed by it all. It was her first major holiday spent with Oliver's family, and her nerves were feeling more frayed the longer it went on. She'd already spent all afternoon repeating her life story to everyone in the family and answering what felt like a million questions about how married life was treating them. Oliver helped a lot, of course, but being the newcomer, a lot of questions were directed at her, specifically. So many names and faces were packed into the humble cabin, and she could hardly remember half of them. All of this piled on top of the pressure she felt to be interesting but not annoying while also being easy-going but not boring. There was that headache, again

Just as she was starting to run through her list of names again, she felt a hand on her shoulder and turned to see it was Oliver. The concern on his face showed that he knew she was feeling overwhelmed but was trying to keep things calm.

"Do you want to step out on the porch for a minute? It may be a good time to cool down."

Claire nodded quickly, grateful for her husband's thoughtfulness, and the two of them grabbed their coats and slipped out the front door. Outside, a chilly breeze immediately made them shiver, but it felt good compared to the oven of a room they had been sitting in. They both breathed in deep and let it out slowly.

"That's better," Claire whispered, feeling her heart settle back into a resting rhythm. She hadn't even realized how fast it had been beating - no wonder she was feeling so jittery.

Oliver quietly walked over and sat on the porch swing that hung nearby, and Claire joined him as he started swinging it slowly back and forth. Everything beyond the warm porch light was completely dark - even the moon and stars were hidden by clouds overhead. It was quiet and peaceful.

Now feeling a little better, Claire asked Oliver to run through his family members again for her.

He smiled, knowingly, and obliged.

"Ok, so there's Uncle Charlie and Aunt Cassie - they're the ones who moved across town recently. Their kids are Hannah, Ben, and Lucy. Hannah just started college, and Lucy just started a new job and lives several hours away, so it's a big deal she was able to make it back for this."

Claire nodded, remembering Aunt Cassie talking about decorating their new house for fall. It sounded like she went all in on that sort of thing.

Oliver continued, "Ben, of course, is their youngest sibling. He always has wild stories that are *incredibly* entertaining. You know he told me he and his friend saw a ghost recently?"

Claire smiled thinking of Ben and how he immediately told her all about his adventure with his friend when they arrived for dinner.

"Of course, you know my parents, Bailey, Sam, and Leo, so that's a big chunk of the names out of the way. Plus, there's Grandma and Grandpa (some of the younger ones call him 'Pa'), who live here."

Claire knew that, of course, but appreciated the refresher. She thought of the few memories she already had with Oliver's family as he talked. She'd appreciated how kind everyone was to her throughout the wedding process earlier that year and even now as they got into the holidays. Despite still feeling a little out of place, they had done a lot to help her feel welcome. Oliver's cousin, Hannah, in particular, had really gone out of her way to make Claire feel like part of the family.

"That just leaves Aunt Jess and Uncle Noah, who live across town. Their kids are Caleb and Blake. Blake just started graduate school this year, around the same age as Lucy and Sam, and Caleb is a Junior in high school, so about the same age as Leo."

"Ok," Claire said, nodding again, "I think I can handle that. More or less."

Oliver smiled and took her hand, "And it's ok if not. It's a lot of people to keep up with, and we aren't going to kick you out or anything."

Claire knew that and said as much, but she was still determined to get it all straight, if not that night then at least by Christmas.

The few minutes outside had already made her feel a lot better, though. She was physically cooling down in the crisp air and was feeling more confident about keeping it all straight in her head after talking it through with Oliver again. Now the warmth of being inside was fully wearing off, and Claire shivered. Oliver put his arm around her and asked if she wanted to go back inside, but she said she needed another minute or two. They huddled together on the swing, and it rocked gently back and forth.

Just then a small speck drifted into the porch light and landed on Oliver's nose. He jerked his head aside, surprised by the sudden attack.

"Was that -"

"Snow!" Claire exclaimed. They looked out as far as the porchlight would allow and saw that flakes were starting to drift to the ground.

Oliver leapt out of the swing and pulled open the front door.

"Hey everyone! It's snowing!"

Several of the cousins immediately piled out of the house, as if they'd never seen snow before, and bounded into the yard as someone inside turned on the floodlights, illuminating the front yard. They ran into the yard and admired the flakes as they got bigger and gracefully floated through the air around them.

Sam and Caleb started throwing a frisbee back and forth that seemed to appear out of nowhere, and some of the younger cousins started playing a game of tag. Most of the older adults stayed inside but watched from the window and out of the opened door, amused at the sudden excitement a little snow could bring. Claire and Oliver joined Sam and Caleb and circled around to throw the frisbee back and forth, mostly throwing it too high or directly into the ground but having fun anyway. Bailey and Ben chased each other around in the snow, lost in their own world.

Aunt Jess hurried outside, shivering as she walked down the steps with her camera.

"Everyone get together! I'm going to take a quick picture!"

The younger ones grumbled quietly about always having to take a picture, but they relented and grouped together.

Click

And with that, everyone went back to what they were doing. For several minutes, despite the general lack of coats in the group, they hardly seemed to notice how cold it had gotten outside, but when Grandma Martha called out that dessert was ready for whoever wanted it, everyone quickly piled inside, all commenting on how nice it was to be out of the cold.

Grandma revealed that she made the apple pie with apples Blake and Caleb had picked recently, and everyone enthusiastically asked for a piece. Grandpa Bill was up now and cutting the pie. Lucy went over and started handing out slices to be passed around on plates. Claire was normally not much of a pie person, but she decided to grab a slice anyway, and she found that she was pleasantly surprised by how much she enjoyed it. She wasn't sure if this was really the case, but she felt like the handpicked apples helped make the pie taste especially good and perfectly sweet.

As everyone was finishing up dessert, Oliver and Claire joined a game at the table in the sun room with Hannah and Caleb. Hannah revealed that she had found the game at a local thrift shop, which prompted Aunt Cassie to talk about her own thrift store haul that she'd gotten recently with her friend, Bianca.

Claire sat and listened as the story prompted others to share some of their own adventures from the past several months. Claire enjoyed their stories of corn mazes, pumpkin carving competitions, and hidden beauty that was discovered in little corners of everyone's lives. Blake even brought out a beautiful, old book that he had apparently borrowed from a local bookshop. Everyone readily jumped in on the excitement, and each story naturally led to the next.

Oliver's parents revealed that they had apparently had quite the experience with a power outage a month or so ago, which brought up Grandma's hidden piano talent. Everyone cheered for her to play a tune, so she settled at the old piano that had recently been moved upstairs and tapped out a gentle, but upbeat, melody that became the soundtrack for the evening. Grandpa Bill was locked in on the mesmerizing movement of her hands as she played, and everyone seemed to relax even more.

For a long time, the room was filled again with laughter and conversation as games continued and music washed over the scene. Pa Bill was sitting in his recliner for a minute, looking like he was fighting sleep induced by the thanksgiving spread from earlier.

As the night waned on, the house was filled with a lively murmur. Nothing could bother the occupants of the log house. At one point, during a particularly lively game, Claire even knocked her drink over on the table, but no one was bothered for even a moment. Rather, they jumped over each other to help clean the mess.

Although slightly embarrassed, Claire was thankful for the good-natured laughter that quickly brushed the event aside. Everyone was so genuinely lighthearted and kind that she almost felt silly for her earlier nervousness. The nerves were still there - they probably would be for a while - but a comfortable feeling joined them, and she felt settled in with Oliver's family for the evening.

Throughout the rest of the evening, Claire found out a lot about where everyone was in life as she talked with them. Through the stories, she found out that most everyone was going through a lot of change. Amazingly, the last few months had also brought a lot of peace for the family, despite all of the transition.

What most struck Claire was that none of the changes were fully settled or over for anyone. Jobs were still new, houses were still difficult, routines were still disrupted, and anxiety was still felt, but slowly and patiently, Autumn gently settled the family into life more than they were before.

The family's stories were full of fantastical details from friendly birds to larger-than-life leaf piles, but Claire saw through the tales to the real center of each story. She realized each one was really about the people around them.

Whether it was friends or family, there was someone in each story who shared the experience, and it was the relationship that made the story worth telling. Now, Claire found herself part of another one of their stories. She knew when they would tell it later, the focus would be on the music or the food or the surprise snowfall outside, but the real thing that they'd all remember the evening for would be each other.

Claire took it all in, thankful for the trust Oliver's family put in her as they shared their stories. Each one was shared freely and enthusiastically, and each elicited laughter and smiles from everyone listening. Claire traded a few of her own as the hours went by, and funnily enough, she found herself feeling pleasantly comfortable. Sharing Autumn tales made her feel at home, and she knew that, although the transition into married life wasn't over yet, it was going to be a lovely journey grounded in the peace of their wonderful relationships.

Before they went home that evening, Claire remembered her notebook that she had left on the floor by the loveseat. Picking it up, she recalled the many stories that had been shared that night and smiled thinking about how poetic it all was. When Oliver asked what had her smiling so big, she simply replied,

"I think I may be getting over my writer's block."

Despite all the worries that could have plagued the evening, everyone found a moment of true rest, even if they knew it might not last forever. Claire still felt the pressure of being the newcomer, of course, but she also felt entrusted with the warmth that came with family and the joy that everyone had found that Fall in change and transition. As she continued to settle into her new life with Oliver, she felt a sense of peace surrounded by his loud, goofy family and even found herself excited for the holidays.

Life may feel chaotic at the best of times, but for now, it was a little clearer to Claire that simple joy and peace were often waiting right around the corner.

Beauty Begs to Be Seen

It screams from rustling leaves
It floods from the sky
It springs from the ground

Blink and you'll miss it
Sunflowers in a corn field
Roses in suburbia
Honey in the treetops

Beauty begs to be seen
Joy begs to be felt
Peace begs to be embraced

We have only to See, Feel, and Embrace

- J.S.

Cozy Autumn Tales

Here, in the Forest, stories like this grow fast and strong. The cool air and soft sun is perfect for cultivating the peace we need at just the right time. When the chaos of life starts to become overwhelming, I always find myself back in this place, thinking of these stories and looking for the hidden beauty and joy around me that I might have missed otherwise. I think of my journey through the Forest and how my family and friends helped me settle into it.

Growing up, my mom would tell me tales of Autumn, and I would always get swept up in the peace and adventure. Over the years I have probably heard dozens of stories from her and the rest of the family. Often, I would ask her to read me her poems, and she would pull out her old notebook from the year her and my dad got married, though she had them all memorized.

Years later, my family still tells stories. There are a lot more now, but occasionally we'd hear old stories about great-grandma Martha playing the piano or my uncles wandering the forest on Thanksgiving, and Aunt Bailey always talked about the leaf piles they made growing up when she came over to help us rake the lawn. Now my mom's poetry recalls deep nostalgia for me as I think about the stories I've heard from generations before me, my own Autumn tales that I've experienced, and the ones that are yet to come.

Every Autumn we all have stories that we live in. Some are reruns of old tales and rituals that have made us who we are over the years, while some are new episodes that form the path ahead of us. Every story brings you to the next, and in Autumn, there's something in the air that helps us slow down a little as we go.

Whether it's exploring hidden gardens or still mountaintops, Fall seems ripe with opportunities to find peace and contentment, lingering just underneath all the noise and chaos of our everyday lives. These places of rest revive us and settle us as we face challenges and transition. These experiences bring us closer together with those around us, and we see each other in a softer light.

As much as I love Fall, the joy of the stories and memories I share during this season isn't just from the experiences themselves, but it's also the retelling of those stories in the times to come. When you're sheltered inside during a Winter snowstorm or being drenched by a Spring rain, those Autumn stories are still yours, and I find they tend to make it easier to find the beauty in the seasons ahead, too.

These stories belong to my family, but they are familiar to many of us. In the years since my mom first joined my dad's family for Thanksgiving, our family has lived out many joyful stories just like these. These stories made me who I am, and, although I often find myself once again wandering the dark jungle, each time I do I feel more confident that I will eventually find my way back to the enchanting forest of warmth and light with the people I care about, and I know that they will be there waiting to welcome me back when I do.

Autumn is a beautiful place to find and cherish our wonderful stories. There's something in the air that begs for peace this time of year. Whether you are feeling the peace of the last Autumn or dreaming of the Autumn to come, I hope you find your garden or orchard to sit in peace, surrounded by life and gentle beauty. May these stories guide and relax you with nostalgia and vivid color.

When Autumn comes for you again, I hope peace is easier for you to find than it was before. When the heat of

Summer gives way to cool breezes and soft light, look for the sunflower in the cornfield or pumpkin in the forest to remind you that growth and life is happening everywhere.

As it often does, Autumn will give us a time to settle into life and embrace the little things that make it beautiful. Truly, this time of year is something special. With any luck, we'll bring a renewed sense of peace and adventure from this season into the next.

For now, whether you're experiencing the coolness of Autumn, the cold of Winter, the heat of Summer, or the growth of Spring, I pray that you find rest and enchanted beauty in unexpected corners of your life. May the flowers be bright, the fruit sweet, the breeze cool, and the Forest quiet and peaceful.

Acknowledgements

I have a lot of people to thank for this book coming together, but ultimately, I must start somewhere different for acknowledgments. This book and these stories were about the enchanting Forest of peace that Autumn so often reveals to us, but for me it's important to talk about the Creator who planted this Forest for us.

Every concept of peace and love in these stories comes from God who supplies us with every good and perfect thing. Without Him and the love that flows from Him into Creation, none of these stories could happen nor could the ones that influenced them from my own life. Finding beauty and peace in the chaos is only truly possible through God and Jesus who came to Earth to bring us the everlasting peace and show us true rest in Him. To really understand any of this, that is most important.

From there, I must mention many people who played specific roles in getting this book together. As I mentioned before, the book is dedicated to my wonderful wife, my parents, and my siblings, and I especially thank Mary Grace and Caleb for taking the time to read this story and help me figure out how to polish it. Your thoughts and support made a huge difference.

Of course, I have to say thank you to the rest of my family. My Mimi and Pa and Grandma and Grandpa were certainly very present as I was thinking about Bill and Martha, and they all made such an impact on how I think about family in my life. That's not the mention all of my aunts and uncles and cousins from both sides of the family who all had an influence on the characters in one way or another as I put the Emberley family together. I am so thankful for all of my family and how they've affected my life.

Then I must thank Jessica, Madison, Lilly, and Jaylee for also reading the book and giving me so much encouragement along the way! You all are great friends, and I am thankful for you.

Of course, that extends to all of our wonderful friends at West End who I have spent the last several Autumns with. You all are the absolute best, and I am so thankful for your presence during my favorite time of year.

I am also very thankful for my in-laws, Jason and Shelli, as well as my wife's siblings, Leslie and Andrew and his wife McCarly. That's not even to mention the rest of the Goldens, the Hutchesons, and the Duncans who welcomed me so warmly to the family when Mary Grace and I got married. All of their influence is in this book as well, and I am very grateful for this new family I had the privilege to become a part of.

Lastly, I am thankful to many of my friends for the many Autumns we have spent together and the incredible influence they've had on my life and subsequently this book.

Thank you, Namon, Caleb and Meghan. In many ways, you all taught me to see the adventure in every day.

Thank you to all of my Harding friends, who I shared many Fall adventures with. I was definitely thinking of each of you and the many experiences we had in Arkansas as I was writing this.

Specifically, thank you Dakota, Jackson, Ethan, Jake, Bryan, and Alberto for so many fun stories.

Finally, I want to say thank you to my favorite band, Dawson Hollow, for the many Fall memories going to concerts and listening while you all perform songs that I consider to make the perfect Autumn soundtrack.

About the Author:

Joshua Shockley lives with his wife in Appalachia and is a professional writer for an electric cooperative, focusing on community news and programs. He also runs a publication on Substack called the Every Day Museum of Art that emphasizes the beauty of everyday life and the power of treating the world around you like an art museum full of art to admire and enjoy. Aside from writing, he also practices several other forms of art including drawing and graphic design (as shown in this book) and film photography. Prints are for sale in his shop on Etsy at the link below!

Buy Art

Instagram

Substack